Spectacular Book!!!

People from a thousand years ago become very real.

You will LOVE reading about Lady Margaret. A word of advice: Don't start this book if you have tasks that must be done. Extremely interesting and powerful. What a talented writer, who is an expert in the time period.

—KINDLE CUSTOMER

What will happen?

This novel brings to life a peripheral character in history and uses her to tell the story of the society in which she lives. I can't wait to read what happens to Lady Margaret next!

—ANNA VORHES

Great Historical Novel!

Through her descriptions of the characters and their surroundings, she paints a picture that makes you think you are there. Having read this prequel, I am anticipating the first book of the trilogy to come out! Very good story!

—SHARON H. LACHAPELLE

Note: This novella includes instances of beatings, murders, and the death of an infant, which may be triggers from some readers.

Also by This Author

Henry's Spare Queen Trilogy:

Lady Margaret's Escape Book One
Lady Margaret's Challenge Book Two
Lady Margaret's Future Book Three

Lady Margaret's Disgrace: Prequel to
Henry's Spare Queen Trilogy
Release Date: 1 September 2021

Find Victoria online and on social media:
Website: *victoriasportelli.com*
Facebook: facebook.com/victoriasportelli/
Pinterest.com/VictoriaSportelli/
Twitter: @SportelliVic

Dear Reader:

The author will be most grateful
if you leave an honest review online.
Thank you!

LADY MARGARET'S
DISGRACE

Prequel to Henry's Spare Queen Trilogy

VICTORIA SPORTELLI

Creazzo Publishing
Sioux Falls, South Dakota

Creazzo Publishing
401 E. 8th Street Suite 214-1194
Sioux Falls, South Dakota 57104
USA

Published by Creazzo Publishing in 2021
Original Copyright © 2018
www.CreazzoPublishing.com

ISBN 978-1-952849-09-1 (paperback)
ISBN 978-1-952849-11-4 (ebook)

Credits:
Cover Design: Jennifer D. Quinlan
Interior Design: www.wordzworth.com
Map and Illustration: Lindsey A. Grassmid
Editor: Margaret K. Diehl

Publisher's Cataloging-In-Publication Data
(Prepared by The Donohue Group, Inc.)
Names: Sportelli, Victoria, author. | Grassmid, Lindsey A., illustrator.

Title: Lady Margaret's disgrace / Victoria Sportelli ; [map and illustration: Lindsey A. Grassmid].
Description: 2nd edition. | Sioux Falls, South Dakota : Creazzo Publishing, 2021. | "Prequel to Henry's Spare Queen Trilogy." | Interest age level: 017-018. | Summary: "In 1099, Lady Margaret is betrothed to the heir of a great Norman estate and is about to become a countess. Before she can wed, her beloved mother dies. After the funeral, Margaret is betrayed by an enemy she did not expect—her father. He claims she traded her honor for pleasures with a lowly Saxon servant. Acting on his lie, Lord Charles declares Margaret his slave ... Margaret believes nothing can save her from a life of servitude, but she is wrong. Soon a king will need her help."–Provided by publisher.

Identifiers: ISBN 9781952849091 (paperback) | ISBN 9781952849114 (ePub)

Subjects: LCSH: Ladies-in-waiting–England–History–To 1500–Juvenile fiction. | Fathers and daughters–England–History–To 1500--Juvenile fiction. | Henry I, King of England, 1068-1135–Juvenile fiction. | Great Britain–History–1066-1687–Juvenile fiction. | Betrayal–Juvenile fiction. | CYAC: Ladies-in-waiting–England–History–To 1500–Fiction. | Fathers and daughters–England–History–To 1500–Fiction. | Henry I, King of England, 1068-1135–Fiction. | Great Britain–History–1066-1687–Fiction. | Betrayal–Fiction. | LCGFT: Historical fiction.

Classification: LCC PZ7.1.S7174 Lad 2021 (print) | LCC PZ7.1.S7174 (ebook) | DDC [Fic]–dc23

For Teri,

Thank you
for convincing me
to write this novella.

Contents

England, 1099 A.D.   viii

Motte and Bailey, Royal Oaks   ix

A Royal Family   x

A Noble Family   xi

Characters   xii

Preface   xv

Chapter 1   Home   1

Chapter 2   A Dance   11

Chapter 3   More Than Dinner   17

Chapter 4   A Death   23

Chapter 5   The Ghost   33

Chapter 6   Refusal   37

Chapter 7   Revelation   41

Chapter 8   Acceptance   47

Chapter 9   Royal Trial   53

Chapter 10   Taxes   57

Chapter 11   Advent   63

Chapter 12   A Late Celebration   69

Chapter 13   Christmastide   73

Chapter 14   Easter Sunday   77

Chapter 15   New Forest   79

Chapter 16   Westminster Abbey, London   85

Chapter 17   Convent of the Black Friars   89

Chapter 18   Royal Oaks, Worcestershire   93

Chapter 19   Loss   99

Chapter 20   Murder   103

Chapter 21   Margaret's Ride   111

Chapter 22   A Plan   117

Author's Note   119

Excerpt from Lady Margaret's Escape   121

Acknowledgements   133

Glossary   134

About the Author   141

England, 1099 A.D.

Motte and Bailey, Royal Oaks

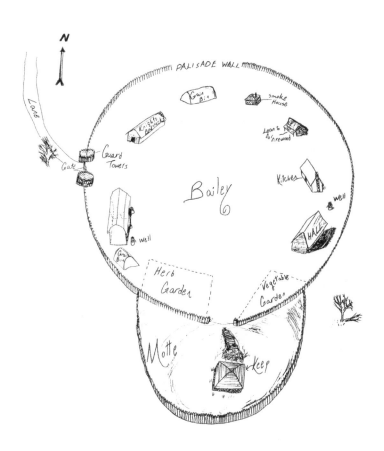

A Royal Family

William I (the Conqueror)   *m.*   **Matilda of Flanders**
b. 1028 - d. 1087 A.D.   b. 1031 - d. 1083 A.D.
King of England 1066 - 1087 A.D.

Children:

Richard (Deceased)

Robert
Duke of Normandy

William II
b. 1056 A.D.
King of England 1088 A.D.

Henry

A Noble Family

Charles   *m.*   **Rosamonde**

b. 1064 A.D.   b. 1069 A.D.

Lord, Royal Oaks Estate-1086

Children:

Margaret

Charles

(called Young Charles)

Raymond

Cecily

Characters

Normans

Edouard, Earl of Three Ridges. His wife is Lady Ridges. His heir is Young Edouard.

Henry de Beaumont, 1st Earl of Warwick. Holds the most lands for the Crown and is the most powerful earl. His immediate support of Henry helped make him King of England.

Lord Artus. Vassal to a baron, who is a vassal to Lord Ridges.

Lord Bardoul. A lord who is a vassal to Lord de Belleme.

Lord Chancellor. An important figure in the royal court who is head of the Norman judiciary system, handles the king's legal matters, holds and protects the royal seal, and oversees the court scribes. He is one of the few noblemen who can read, write, and figure because he is also a priest.

Lord Charles of Royal Oaks. His estate lies three days' ride north of Gloucester in Worcestershire

Robert de Belleme: 3rd Earl of Shropshire and Shrewsbury. Holder of those and several other estates; the most powerful lord in England after the Earl of Warwick.

Sir Bruis. Knight-errant in service to Lord Charles of Royal Oaks.

Sir Ignace. Knight-errant in service to Lord Charles of Royal Oaks.

William I (the Conqueror), formerly Duke of Normandy. Married
Matilda of Flanders. Invaded England in 1066 A.D., had himself
crowned King and ruled England until he died in 1087.

Children: **Richard** died in a hunting accident.

Robert was passed over for the English crown and accepted the
Dukedom of

Normandy. In 1097 he joined the Grand Crusade to the Holy Land
in search of weatlth.

William II (Rufus) was his father's favorite son.

Henry holds land and great wealth in Normany inherited from his
mother.

Clergy

Anselm, Archbishop of Canterbury. An important monk and
theologian. In England he defended the Catholic Church's inter-
ests. He has been exiled by King William II since 1097.

Father Ambroise. Priest on Sir Charles's Royal Oak's estate.

Gerard, Bishop of Hereford. Appointed by King William I as his
Lord Chancellor, he also served King William II. When Anselm,
Archbishop of Canterbury, was refused re-entry to England after
a visit to the pope, Gerard assumed some of Anselm's duties for
the remaining bishops.

William Giffard, Bishop of Winchester. Nominated to his position
3 August 1100 by Henry; probably due to Henry's efforts to
win Church support for his claim to the English throne and to
reward Giffard for his support.

Saxon

Aldrich. Farmer, village elder and a former reeve of Lord Charles' estate.

Cook. Head person in a kitchen who supervised a staff of bakers, undercooks, scullery maids, men, and other persons needed to feed everyone inside the bailey.

Fearn. Fourteen, Lord Charles' latest bedmate

Goda. Aldrich's wife.

Holen. A Saxon woman.

Jorgon. Ten, a stable boy for Lord Charles.

Jorgon Elder. Jorgon's father and a villein on Lord Charles' estate.

Reeve. The title of the Saxon leader elected by the Saxon men for a one-year term. He assigns common land for planting and decides all other matters among the Saxons. He reports to his lord's seneschal or to the lord himself.

Other

Aegdyth. Princess of Scotland and sister to King Domnall; later renamed Matilda.

Caitlin. Irish. Brought to London to be sold as a slave, bought by Lord Charles as a wedding gift for his bride. She has been the nursemaid to Lady Margaret since her birth.

Domnall, King of Scotland. Also known as Donald Bane and King Donald III.

Preface

In 1066 C.E., after invading and subjugating England's people, William the Conqueror (King William I) ruled until 1087. He did not want his son Robert to become the next King of England so he made William, his third son and favorite, his heir. William I awarded Prince Robert his lands, property, wealth in Normandy and his title, Duke of Normandy. In turn, Robert gave his word to relinquish all claims to the English crown. Prince Robert, now also the Duke of Normandy, appeared pacified, but he was not.

Crowned in 1088 C.E., King William II made three drastic and unpopular changes. He razed sixty-five houses and shops in Winchester to build a new castle. Next, William created his personal hunting grounds for deer and wild boar by requiring several earls and lords leave their prosperous estates southwest of Winchester and move elsewhere. He razed all they had built, planted trees and renamed the area New Forest. King William II established three courts a year, Easter in Gloucester, Michaelmas in London, Christmas in Winchester, and he required every baron and earl to appear at each court to re-pledge his fidelity and to hear King William's latest decrees.

Henry, William's younger brother, had inherited great wealth from his mother. While his lands were in Normandy, Henry spent much of his time in England. He learned to speak Saxon, became acquainted with the Saxons and their customs, and listened to the concerns and complaints of many landholders.

In 1097, King William II denied the right of Anselm, Archbishop of Canterbury, to replace deceased bishops and took the incomes from those lands for himself. Archbishop Anselm removed his support of King William II and left England for Rome to seek counsel from Pope Urban II. When Anselm asked to return to England, William refused him entry.

By 1099, King William II had ruled England for eleven years. The king's actions had angered the bishops. Many barons, earls, and lords wondered if King William might take their lands for more income as he had taken the Church's. At Easter, the king presented his brother Henry to the Court, but the prince did not meet Lord Charles of Royal Oaks.

During Easter Court 1099, Lord Charles contracted to marry his daughter Margaret to the heir of Edouard, Earl of Three Ridges. A most persuasive man, the earl forced Lord Charles to give a huge dowry to his least favorite child for the privilege of her becoming a countess. Frustrated and resentful, Lord Charles blamed his wife Rosamonde for the coin he was about to lose. Upon arriving home, he began his schemes of revenge.

1

Home

20 April 1099

Lady Margaret enjoyed the coziness of the kitchen shed as she sipped a mug of hot vegetable broth. She watched Cook turn from stirring the pot over the fire to step to the work table to inspect hot loaves of bread. Margaret inhaled the warm, yeasty smell. Because the bottom half of the door was closed, a servant was visible only to her waist.

"My lady? The hall is ready for your inspection," she reported as she curtseyed so only her head showed.

Margaret placed her empty cup on a window ledge and took up her bag of herbs.

"Thank you, Cook."

The woman only harrumphed.

Margaret closed the half door and stepped away. She bent to pet Yolo, her father's favorite hunting dog, and the other two in turn. With a wave, she shooed them off and surveyed the compound.

Yard swept. Garden weeded. Firewood replenished. Laundry taken in from the line. The guard walking the wall and the one standing beside the gate are relaxed. Not yet in sight. We are ready. This time will he be pleased with me?

As she walked from the kitchen shed to the long building, Margaret craned her neck to admire the hall's newly thatched roof. Rather than use the formal entrance, she slipped through the closer, servants' door. She smelled the fire and felt the spring of new rushes under her feet. The table atop the dais was set for seven, the family and Father Ambroise. Three short candles on wooden circles lit the table. At each place set a wooden bowl on a wooden plate, a pewter spoon to the right and a pottery mug above the tip of the spoon. Each diner used the dagger he or she wore for personal use as a dinner knife as well.

She nodded her approval to the page, who had pulled his forelock to show his respect for a lady of the manor. Margaret looked right. The fire pit down the center of the building had been lit to remove the chill. Margaret smiled because the servants remembered to use so little wood.

Father cannot complain I am being wasteful. Will he notice how I obey his wishes? Thank me for it this time? Expect it not. Never has before. Will he ever smile at me like when I was little? Oh, I do hope so.

As Margaret walked down one side of the pit and up the other, she sprinkled freshly cut rosemary and dried herbs to scent the new rushes covering the dirt floor. She inspected between the posts that held up the roof; each stall was ready to hold the knights' armor, swords, and gear. The barrel of ale and a table of empty pitchers were in place. Trestle tables with benches under them faced the fire pit so the diners could warm their feet as they ate. The side table by the front entrance was stacked with the wooden dinnerware: bowls, dinner slabs, spoons, mugs.

Returning to the dais, Margaret turned to give the space a final inspection.

"Well done," she told the work crew. "You are excused for now."

"Thank you, my lady," they intoned as they gave obeisance and departed.

Hearing voices beyond the main entrance, she walked to the front of the hall and listened behind the closed door.

"We wait on the palisade walkway to the left of the gate and wave as they return," she heard her brother Charles say.

Before she could op the door and join her siblings, they were gone. Margaret sighed and left for the servants' entrance. *Dare I join them? Will they be pleased? Push me off the walkway? That fall may break my back. Better not. Wait by the door.*

Lord Charles of Royal Oaks rode ahead of his wife and their knights. The party filed out of the oaks that ringed their estate and toward their compound. Leaves rustled in a gentle breeze. They rode down the lane bound on either side by sweet-smelling fields of green and yellow. Spring was lush with the promise of a bountiful harvest to come. Sir Charles's stiff back and refusal to look neither right nor left bespoke his anger. The field workers still curtseyed or pulled their forelocks as he passed. The villeins knew they had best step lightly and stay out of his way—again. Looking toward the entry gate of the bailey, Sir Charles glared at the guards and his offspring.

The children on the palisade walkway stopped waving and looked at each other. They dashed to the ladder. Standing by the servants' door at one end of the long wall, Margaret saw them scurrying toward the main door at the other end of the wall.

Something is wrong, she thought. *At least this time not something I did or did not do.*

She removed her apron and passed it and the bag of herbs to the servant behind her. The wench disappeared. Margaret was pleased her pale yellow bliaut was still clean; she admired her favorite border trim of blue and green lines in squares. Each center held a different embroidered flower. Of course, in the center box held a yellow center surrounded by white petals, her favorite flower.

Margaret looked at her hem. *My first border. Mother made it for me when I was born.* Margaret smoothed down her skirt and tucked a loose lock behind her left ear. She turned her face to the gentle breeze, lifted her face to the setting sun and smiled. At the other end of the building, two boys and a girl formed a reception line.

Still not part of their group. Never will be. He favors them, never me. No matter how hard I try. When will this end?

Margaret's siblings had lined up without leaving a space for her. She sighed as she looked at the cloudless pale sky. The sun would soon set behind the Keep in the southwest corner of the bailey. That and the Hall would put the group in shadow. Margaret frowned, marched toward them, and pushed Cecily aside to stand after her brothers. Cecily shoved back but stopped when she spotted her father riding through the gate followed by the roundseys carrying a litter. The youngest child smoothed the bell sleeves of her new green bliaut, grabbed her skirt to straighten it and preened. Margaret looked to her father and stiffened her shoulders.

His eyes! Something is very wrong.

Lady Rosamonde was hidden by the curtains of the litter her husband had forced her to use. She could not leave the conveyance until the group stopped.

Have they been quarreling again? Is Mother safe?

Margaret did not have to look at her sister to know Cecily was preening and wriggling with excitement. After Sir Charles dismounted, he gave curt, clipped orders, and turned away from the column. As Lord Charles walked toward his children, a knight helped Lady Rosamonde out of the litter.

Young Charles, the elder boy, bowed first and used a formal tone. "Welcome home."

Raymond did the same.

Each was greeted with only a nod.

"Welcome home, Father," said Margaret softly as she curtseyed low.

"Father!" exclaimed Cecily as she bobbed a short curtsey and reached for him.

Sir Charles smiled and grasped her little hands in his giant ones. "I have missed your sunny smile, daughter. Charles, Raymond, come with us."

The boys walked behind him; Lord Charles held Cecily's hand as she chattered at him. Margaret stood alone and ignored as they entered the Hall. Her eyes stung.

Lady Rosamonde arrived and hugged her first-born. The woman sucked in a deep breath and sighed aloud. Her shoulders relaxed.

At least you still love me. Margaret hugged back hard. For a moment she laid her head on her mother's chest and inhaled the smell of lavender, love and comfort.

Lady Rosamonde stroked her daughter's wavy hair at the crown and down her back. "Smells clean. You washed it for Easter, I see."

Margaret raised her head and smiled. *I know I may not speak prideful things, but my wavy hair is beautiful.* "The ends are now at my knees."

5

"And soon the summer sun will streak your warm brown with golden highlights, my beautiful daughter."

"Thank you, Mother." *You always know when I need a compliment or a bit of praise.*

Lady Rosamonde leaned forward and whispered, "I bought you a cube of lavender-scented soap for your next hair washing."

One for Cecily, or she will whine to Father; then he will take it from me. "And one for Cecily?"

"And one for Cecily. I have been so looking forward to seeing you, my dearest. Help me unpack. I have news." With an arm around Margaret's shoulders, Lady Rosamonde walked her daughter around the end of the Hall and up the steps toward the Keep. They proceeded up the entry ladder and to the third floor where Lord Charles and his wife lived.

Please, God, let it be good news. Mayhap, time away from this place and his glaring at me.

While Margaret waited for her mother to speak, she admired her mother's trim figure and graceful movements as she turned about the room to ease her muscles after a long day of reclining in a swaying litter.

I understand not. Why does Father ignore you? Be angry when you bring home coins from our midwifery? Why do you two sneer at each other? What happened?

After servants had delivered the trunks, Margaret found her mother's slippers and helped her into them. She scraped mud from Rosamonde's travel boots into the fire in the brazier. She brushed them clean and polished their dullness with a rag. To chase the chill in the room, Margaret placed more small pieces of wood in the two braziers set on metal tripods. She checked that the floor around each brazier was clear of rushes. Even one spark could set them aflame and the wooden building would burn. She stood back and watched her mother unpack, shake out her clothes, and hang them on their pegs.

"Did you wear them all at Court?"

Rosamonde turned and smiled. "Yes, but I set aside the pale blue for Easter Sunday." Rosamonde continued to talk as she worked. "After eleven years as king, one would think William Rufus would feel secure. Yet, he requires his lords to attend all three courts every year and to re-pledge their allegiance. I think he trusts not any one of them." With one hand, Rosamonde held aloft her matching pale blue mantle and with the other brushed down a crease. Muttering half to herself and half to Margaret, she voiced her thought. "Why he invited the wives to Gloucester, I am unsure. He neither acknowledged nor spoke to any of us." She paused and then added, "Unless it was to demonstrate further power over his vassals." She hung the garment on its peg.

"Will you attend again?"

"I doubt he will want women in London at Michaelmas or Winchester for Christmas. At least I hope not."

Margaret kept her thoughts to herself as she helped her mother out of her brown traveling bliaut and into a better one, her clean cream-colored one, and gave her the brown girdle. From her own waist girdle, she handed over her mother's set of household keys and the only scissors on the estate. *Holidays are much happier with Father gone; I will have Mother. Thank you, King William!*

Now dressed to sup, Rosamonde turned to her daughter and motioned her to the stools behind them. In unison they sat beside the brazier. Smiling at her beloved parent, Margaret waited. *News. Please be good.*

"We leave soon. In ten days we travel to attend Lady Liane for her third lying-in and birthing." Rosamonde grinned to see her daughter's eyes spark and light. "I have two more commissions after that. We may be gone until summer's end." Rosamonde easily read her daughter's mind, but she did not smile.

All summer! No brothers teasing. No sister falsely whining I have pinched her or pulled her hair. No sudden punishments from Father over I know not what. Mother will let me ride Night. Free to ride Night! To appear calm Margaret placed one hand on her lap and lay the other over it as she pushed back her shoulders and straightened her spine.

"Good news, I know, but I have more."

What could be better than freedom?

"Recall you the Ridges estate? The first time I took you with Caitlin and me? Six years ago?"

"Was that when I learned to ride Night, and you let me see my first birthing?"

Rosamonde nodded. Then she smiled.

"Their eldest son was away being fostered. He is home now and of an age to marry."

Finally betrothed? Please let it be that!

Rosamonde saw Margaret inhale and hold her breath, so she ran her next comments together. "At Court I met Lady Ridges. Remember, she gave me my first commission and recommended me to others. I have always liked her. She said, 'My son is of an age.' Then I said, 'My Margaret is as well.' Soon we agreed: her son; my daughter. We sent our husbands together. We have a contract."

Air whooshed out of Margaret. "I am finally to be married?" *Thank you, God!*

"Your father will announce it when he is ready."

"What rank?"

"When he inherits, Young Edouard will make you a countess."

A countess! Highest rank, just under the royals. "And his property?"

"Three great estates, one in Normandy and two here. One north of us and the one east, which you have seen. You can visit home when you travel between them."

I will never return. Never will I ask him to visit here. You will have to visit me and stay long. "How soon may I leave?" she asked.

"Oh, my darling girl, I am not eager to lose you so soon!"

"But I should have been betrothed three years ago. I was supposed to go to his family to have his mother teach me how to be the estate chatelaine, like you are here. I must be trained by Lady Ridges to the ways of their households before I am bedded. With three estates to manage, I will have much to learn. May I please go now, Mother? Please! I am almost too old already."

Rosamonde leaned back, so Margaret knew the answer. "If childbirth does not kill you... Oh, daughter, life is so short. I am thirty; your father is thirty-five. We have but five, or at most ten years left of our lives."

Margaret could not imagine her mother's death. She was so strong, so central to her world. Secretly, Margaret was convinced her mother would see fifty, mayhap longer. *Saying so will not advance my cause. Oh, how I will miss you! But I must go now or I fear I will never wear the banded sleeves of a married woman on my bliauts.* "I should have been betrothed at the regular time. I should have been bedded by now and had my first-born, so you might dandle at least one grandchild on your knee before God takes you."

Margaret was breathless with longing. *To be away! To have my own life!* Whatever *Lady Ridge's son is like, he will be better than Father.*

I will not fight with him as Mother does Father. I will be a good, obedient wife and he will like me. We will be happy together. I know it.

"You are my only ally, daughter. I do not wish to part with you."

Margaret heard the tremble in her voice as she said, "Please, Mother. It is my time. Past it."

Lady Rosamonde looked away. "Mayhap at the end of summer. One more summer with you."

Margaret felt heaviness in her chest, a flicker of anger at her beloved parent. She frowned. *You will delay me yet again and say, "Mayhap in the spring." Dear God, when will I get away? Why won't she understand my need for a life away from here?*

Margaret dropped her chin to her chest and slouched her shoulders. Rosamonde moved to the edge of her seat. She wriggled a finger under her first-born's chin and raised the girl's eyes to hers. "I will not part with you any sooner than I must."

2

A Dance

20 April

As Sir Charles's party wended its way homeward from Easter Court in Gloucester, Henry, younger brother of King William II, dashed toward southwest of Southhampton. He prayed the Abbess of Romesy Convent would permit him to visit his beloved for their first semi-annual meeting of the year.

Having left his men and his weapons outside, Henry silently paced the dirt floor of the visitor's chamber, a wooden outbuilding butting against the stones of the outside wall. At each turn, he gazed at the closed convent entrance. The squat, windowless square was lit by fat candles on pedestals in each corner. He positioned himself between a brace of candles, so the woman he awaited would stand in light.

Stopping to stare at a candle, Henry remembered the sunny day he had ridden to the edge of a meadow and watched six girls playing

11

tag among the flowers of the meadow. He remembered thinking they were convent novices; then he wondered about the girl without a wimple. Hair of spun gold flew behind her as she dashed about. When she stopped, Henry noted a comely profile. He could still recall how his heart had thundered at the sight of her. A novice called a warning, and the girl turned. Henry sucked in his breath. For a moment she froze, stately, regal. Then she dashed for the wimple she had dropped.

Henry smiled, recalling her standing her ground when he spurred his horse to her. Their first encounter was burned into his mind. "Who are you?" he had asked. Breathless, she answered, "A novice." Then she tied the white wimple around her head. "No, you are a lady of rank. I am Henry, brother to the king." "Then you should know who I am," she countered. "But you must ask at the convent. I will tell you not." Her smile warmed his whole body. Then she lifted her nose and turned away. Undaunted by her haughty manner, Henry had followed the group to the convent. Her hips swayed as she walked away, and Henry swore he would have her. In the cold waiting room, Henry coughed and his memory faded. He awaited Aegdyth, the only woman he had ever wanted to marry.

As before, he was nervous at seeing his beloved under such close supervision. He pulled up his pale gray hose and pulled down his dark gray tunic. After straightening his belt, he used both hands to run his fingers through his black hair forehead to nape. He sighed at having to wait. He cautioned himself to speak in the code they had developed over the years, polite conventions to obscure their true feelings from others. As she entered with three nuns behind her, the candlelight flickered. They wore white wimples, dark gray gowns and black veils.

Aegdyth wore a white veil. Her sun-colored hair hung loose to her knees, showing she was still a maid. While the veil bespoke that she might have joined the convent, her wearing her own clothes announced otherwise. The pale blue of her linen shift edged her sleeves and the slit neckline of her deep blue bliaut. Golden threads woven into the girdle around her waist emphasized her wealth, and their pattern of Scots thistles with green leaves announced her heritage and rank.

Henry peered into her bright eyes and admired her pale skin. He noted she kept her lips drawn tight instead of loose and in a smile.

Henry bowed low and said, "My lady" with great courtesy and even greater feeling. His eyes never left her face. "Does she see that my ardor has not waned?" he wondered. "Does she still refuse the Scots suitors her brother insists she marry?"

His grin showed her how happy he was to be in her presence, how grateful he was she still wore the white veil of a novice. To the world she appeared to be considering a contemplative life, but really she was a guest who paid well to remain safe from the world of men.

"My lord," said Aegdyth with equal politeness as she curtseyed to him as low as he had bowed. She could not stop her blue-green eyes from drinking him in. She still thought him the handsomest, most forceful man she had ever met. Again, the invisible strength and power within him washed over her. If only she could melt into his arms. She sucked in her breath at the power of her yearning to become his wife. She forced herself to repeat in her mind her plan to become a queen or die a maid. Her heart quieted, yet she still yearned for a future with him.

Thus began the careful dance between a couple separated by circumstances beyond their control. A prince of England desired the princess of Scotland, but he could not marry without his brother King William's permission, which he knew he would never have. She refused to marry one who would not make her a queen as her mother had been.

"I have come from Easter Court."

What he meant was that he had raced to her as soon as his brother had released him.

"Any news of import to the convent?" She was asking for herself, not the sisters.

"Nothing of note. How fares your brother, the king?"

"Again, Domnall wants me home to marry a lord he has chosen for me. My first suitor died; I am in no hurry to accept another. I wrote him I choose to remain here. For the nonce."

Aegdyth looked away and flicked an imaginary mote from her skirt. She sounded casual, even uncaring. Henry knew otherwise. His heart leapt to his throat at hearing those last three words. That his eyes shone told his love he knew her meaning. Her movement had placed her face in shadow so her expression could not be seen by the nuns. Grateful he understood her, she smiled.

Henry thought of the wasted five years they could have been married and the children they could have had by now. He wondered how much longer Aegdyth would wait for him. With William still unmarried and with no heir, he should be the next king of England, but he did not know when.

"And your days?" asked Henry.

"The same. We spend them in prayer and good works. I labor in the garden. And you?"

"I oversee my lands in Normandy. When I am here, I do the king's bidding. I ride about as well."

She understood his restlessness and envied him his freedom. As a princess she required protection. Leaving for any reason would subject her to kidnapping and ransom, even being ravished and forced to marry. Law and custom restrained her. Aegdyth wished she too was free. Wistfully, she admitted to a desire to run in the meadow as she had so long ago. The thought she should have jumped behind him and run away with him that day flashed into her mind. She admitted to herelf, "The time has past when I can do that. I must wait and pray he will be mine." Aegdyth tilted her head and gave him a small sigh.

"I am for Normandy now. I shall not be back until Christmas Court."

"Mayhap I shall see you after that."

"Mayhap you will."

The way Henry emphasized each word told Aegdyth he hoped she would permit him to visit the only other time during the year he was allowed to see her.

"I shall pray for you."

"She means she will wait for me still!" he reasoned.

Relief flooded Henry's heart, but he dared not smile.

"I am grateful for your prayers, and I shall pray for you."

"We go on as before," she thought as she raised her brows a bit to show her agreement.

In unison Henry and Aegdyth gave each other the tiniest nods and the smallest of smiles, the only gifts they could bestow. He bowed as she curtseyed. Their dance ended.

The princess of Scotland reluctantly turned away. Within two steps, the nuns followed her and blocked Henry's view of his love's departure. The convent's heavy outer door closed and heavy bars slammed onto their metal brackets. England's prince stepped forward to put his ear against the wood until he no longer heard the women's footsteps. Henry kissed his fingertips and placed his hand upon the door before he turned away. Lonely and forlorn, Henry crossed that small space and again left his beloved.

3

---- ❧ ----

More Than Dinner

20 April

Four days after Easter Court had ended, three men sat with their feet plopped at the edge of a huge hearth. Two knew better than to refuse the powerful Robert de Belleme's casual invitation to join him. Staring at the crackling fire or into their after-dinner goblets, the earl's guests sat to his left and waited for him to begin. The fire lit the half-circle of chairs before the hearth; the rest of the room was all shadows and gloom.

"How dare he flaunt his sodomite lover before us!" began the Earl of Shropshire and Shrewsbury.

His guests remained mute. They had heard that rumor before. Lord Bardoul silently considered, "Men who dislike like the king create sordid untruths they pass along to sully his name. He enjoys being the king too much to share the throne with a queen." Lord Artus sipped his goblet and kept his eyes on the fire. Their host was too powerful for them to have refused his invitation to accompany him to one of his estates after Easter Court. Now they were being plied with attention, a feast and fine wine. But toward what purpose?

"Bad enough that bastard arrived in Winchester at Christmas Court. Now he openly sleeps in the same bed as the king! An abomination!" continued Belleme.

They had seen his temper before and maintained their silence.

"Now I understand why Rufus refuses to wed. He is a sodomite! The talk I have heard is true."

Each man surmised the earl may well have started the rumors himself. No one had seen the man enter or leave the king's rooms. Mayhap they were only good friends.

"Thrice each year he runs us from Gloucester to London to Winchester to hear his piddling decrees and to re-pledge our fidelity. He has insulted the realm thrice. First, he will not provide an heir; then he displaced loyal men from rich estates so he could expand that bit of woods he has the effrontery to call New Forest. Now he defies the Church and has denied entry to Archbishop Anselm so he can appoint new bishops. For two years he has taken the income from those Church properties for himself."

Lord Bardoul heard his host build a case against the king. He was cert he was hearing treason. Cautious, Lord Artus asked, "What might this portend?" He shifted in his chair so as to avoid seeing the earl's face. That Belleme hated King William was obvious to both men.

"Who knows what he will attempt next? Find a pretext to accuse you of a high crime and take your lands," warned the earl. "The king so viciously put down the lords' rebellion of '95 that now he fears no one. These times, none dare think of rebellion or say a word of defiance for fear of beheading. He should be stopped from his latest outrages, but can he be?"

"Defy the king and you die of treason," reasoned Lord Bardoul. "Then he takes your lands and income and sells them to the richest bidder. He wants to complete that new castle he is building in Winchester. He is capable of anything."

Belleme continued, "That heavy tax in '96 to fund Sir Robert's voyage to the Grand Crusade struck all of England hard. He gained control of his brother's Norman properties. All we got was hardship and suffering, years of them. Ten thousand marks! I, for one, have still not recovered from that outrage."

Both guests thought that to be a lie, but said nothing.

"Should he attempt to tax us like that again, he may well face a revolt," their host warned.

Artus felt his skin crawl. The wine in his mouth turned bitter, but he had to swallow it. Artus wondered if he were sitting between traitors, and if he were expected to join them. Despite the fire at his feet, he was suddenly cold. Belleme was his overlord, but he knew he dare not follow him. He had his family to protect.

"I do not want my son to lose his inheritance over any act of which I might be accused," Lord Artus said. "He is only ten and I must protect what is mine."

Lord Artus's chair scraped against the stone floor as he stood to leave the comforts of the fireplace.

"I am for home, My Lord. I have heard none of this. I know not any of this business nor of anything whatever. My lord, I thank you for the fine dinner, but I must away."

Artus bowed to the pair and strode out of the room. He closed the door silently.

Bardoul decided to join forces with the second most powerful baron in the realm. He asked, "Dare we trust him?"

"No."

"How do we manage him?"

"We both accuse him of conspiring against the king. We both say we heard him. When he accuses us instead, we both swear our fealty. The king may hold a trial or order one of us to a trial by combat. With either course, he dies. Then we both are safe."

That Lord Belleme said 'we both' three times reminded Bardoul of Judas's betraying the Christ three times.

Lord Bardoul shook his head once at how casually the earl could destroy an honorable man and then he stopped himself. He realized if he ever left, he too would die. Belleme had just backed him into a treacherous corner. Stay and risk death for treason. Leave and join Artus' demise. Deciding to avoid sure death, Bardoul chose conspiracy. He promised himself never to cross the man sitting beside him.

The earl spoke as if he had not noticed his guest's reaction, as if he had not guessed his thoughts. But the tiny smile on his thin lips suggested otherwise.

"I will tell William Rufus of Artus's distaste at seeing his 'friend' at Court. I will say Lord Artus said he did not warrant being king. Called him a name I will not repeat to His Majesty."

"I am party to killing a good man," thought Bardoul in dismay. "Soon I will be expected to do worse." He felt a moment's doubt; then his mind steadied. "Become accustomed now or die," he admitted to himself.

"If that does not infuriate the king, I will add that I fear the man might be planning treason, plotting to rid the realm of His Majesty. The king will become enraged and act."

"Good plan," said Bardoul with false conviction. He sipped his wine to keep from having to say more.

"Accomplishes two things. Rids us of possible exposure and treachery. Takes the fertile soil of discontent and sows seeds of rebellion."

The Earl of Shropshire and Shrewsbury thought aloud as he stared at the flames that warmed him. "It will catch hold in others' minds. Men who hate Rufus's rule, who want another king. If his father can conquer a nation, then another man can steal it from his son."

"Are you that man and already plotting?" Bardoul wondered how many men already stood with the earl.

Robert de Belleme looked over the lip of his goblet at his co-conspirator and winked.

Bardoul smiled back because he was expected to do so. He hoped it was convincing. He looked from Belleme to the fire that warmed him not. He fixed his smile to hide the icy shiver coursing down his spine. As he glanced behind him at the dark end of the room, a log falling in the fireplace startled him.

4

A Death

25 April

Five days after her parents' return home, Margaret was at her needlework while seated on a stool in the sunshine. She leaned her back against the Hall wall. Deciding the broidering she had started when she was seven was inferior, she had cut off the first two feet of her wedding rib. That gave her but a yard and a half of acceptable work.

I must sew faster if I am to have this band ready to stitch on my wedding bliaut. She lifted her work to shine in the sun and admired her stitching of the past four days. Two feet of white petals around a yellow center depicted the flower that was her name in Norman, a marguerite. Margaret set the strip on her lap. With the flowers already sewn, she picked up green wool and threaded it through her mother's needle.

After my bedding, my husband's family will award me mine own needle, so written in my marriage contract, says Mother. I will bestow it upon my first-born daughter when she comes of age to sew her wedding rib. If she arrives first, I will treat her better than I have been.

Margaret turned back the edges of the linen strip and flipped it over so only the finished side showed. That left three inches for her pattern of undulating flowers. She admired her stitchery. *Mother said to sew the leaves first, but I think not. Sew the stems flowing from flower to flower then add the leaves in good places.*

On Margaret's cream-colored wedding bliaut, she would sew the decorated rib around the cuff of each sleeve that fit to her elbow and then flared to her wrist. Then another piece would trim the neckline and slit. Finally, a band of wedding rib would encircle the hem of her flared skirt.

If I sew fast enough, I may also have enough to band the front of my matching mantle. Once the priest blesses us at the church door, we will attend our first Mass together. Then my husband will bed me—whatever that means. Lying down together? Sleeping in the same bed? Something else? Our three-step marriage will be complete, contract, blessing, bedding. Afterward, I may band every bliaut and mantle to announce I am a married woman. I will wear my hair in two braids; no one but my husband will ever see my loosed hair again.

Margaret started a stem flowing from flower to flower. *My lord, Edouard the Younger, is comely, Mother says. He will not be like Father, always angry and drinking too much ale at every meal. He will be a good man, like his father. I remember Lord Ridges was polite to me, even though I was still a child.*

Margaret reassured herself anew. *I will bow low when I meet my lord and glance away. My modesty will impress him. Be agreeable to everyone and obey his mother. That will please him. I will meet him soon. Soon I will be with his family.*

A servant interrupted her musings.

"My lady, you must attend your mother. She has taken very ill."

Margaret dumped everything into her sewing basket, stood, and spun about.

"Caitlin?"

"With her. She sends for you."

Margaret raced around the corner of the hall and up the grassy stairs. Her heels pounded on the boards as she ran. She climbed the ladder to the Keep door, dashed across the sitting room and tore up two flights of stairs. She knelt beside her mother's bed and grasped her hand. It was cool.

"Mother, was it anything you ate at dinner?" *Why does your breath smell so bad?*

Rosamonde closed her eyes and rasped, "Poison. He has poisoned me. I know it."

Margaret looked past her mother to her nursemaid; Caitlin shrugged.

"Mayhap it was only a bit of bad food, Mother. Toss it and you will feel better."

"She already has," offered Caitlin. "Still she worsens."

Rosamonde opt her eyes as she squeezed her beloved daughter's hand. Slowly, she turned her head to her child.

"Swear. Swear you will do all I say. Swear!"

Frightened, Margaret agreed, "I swear, Mother."

"If you cannot find Jorgon, find his father. Tell him 'Do as we planned.' Both know what it means." Rosmonde gasped and clutched at her stomach. She thought she would retch; she did not. The afflicted woman continued, "When you do, give Jorgon or Jorgon Elder my pale blue mantle, scarf and gloves. Swear."

"I swear."

"My best hair brush and my both my blue and my green linen bliauts, their shifts, including the mantles and matching shoes, are yours. Put them in your marriage chest now." Rosamonde moaned and rolled to her side.

"Mother?"

"Leave. Get away. To Lady Ridges as soon as possible. Be safe. Be brave, my darling girl. I am dying. Do not linger. Get far away from home." Rosamonde grimaced.

"Caitlin, remain with her. Protect her for me."

Again Rosamonde moaned and grabbed at her belly. "Get the priest. I need the priest."

Margaret dashed down the stairs.

Wearing her hair in a single braid to show she was in mourning, Margaret walked into Mass in a fog. No longer caring for rank or her place in her family, she remained behind. In Margaret's grief at losing the anchor of her life, she could not bring herself to leave the comfort of the church.

Caitlin caught her arm in hers and whispered, "You must stop crying during the service and all the day long. We buried her eleven days ago. Your mother would not want you in this state."

"I will try to do better." Margaret sighed and wiped her eyes. Again this morning Margaret had awakened in her bed next to the drowsy Cecily and listened for her mother's steps, her mother's whisper telling her to rise. She realized she would never again hear the sound of her mother's voice; the tears would not stop.

"Before we break our fasts, we will look on Holen's newborn. This one lived, and you helped her deliver it. That should cheer you."

Margaret tried to smile at her nursemaid. "Yes, Caitlin." Margaret wiped her eyes with her sleeve. *Do not cry. Do not cry or Holen will think something is wrong with her babe. Oh, Mother, we had such times traveling together, sharing the joy of delivering babes together. Never again. I needs to stop being seen crying. Cry only at night and in my bed.*

The wooden Hall, which could accommodate all Lord Charles' retainers and villeins, stood at the south end of the bailey. Huge beams and poles supported the roof twenty feet above the ground. The horizontal boards of the exterior walls had been pegged to the beams and poles. Margaret looked up from her feet, realized they were going to the Hall and cared not. *Do not look for her stool on the dais. He has already removed it and filled the hole with Cecily's. How could he do that?*

Between the upright logs, the stall spaces held extra sacks of grain, the latest barrel of ale, and the knights' weapons and gear when they dined. Trestles, table boards and benches filled three stalls when not in use. The main entrance was on the northwest corner and opposite the dais inside. Behind the raised platform were two storerooms. Leaning against one corner was the ladder that led to the wooden floor above where visitors slept. Two holes in the top of the roof let out the smoke from the fire pit that lay fourteen feet down the center of the room. The family sat on the dais as they did at every meal. Sitting on one end, Margaret pushed her food around the wooden bowl with a wooden spoon. She ate little and heard none of the conversations of her siblings and father. Not even the agreeable smells of the pottage enticed her to poke a morsel of meat with her knife and bring it to her mouth.

At the center of the dais, Sir Charles downed another mug of ale and began constructing his usual mental list of Margaret's faults. He needed them in order to be angry with her again and to work up the courage to do as he had planned. Charles reminded himself of the time Margaret stopped him from beating a Saxon boy. How she had embarrassed him in the middle of the bailey for all to see. To punish her, he broke his promise to her to teach her to ride. When she mounted Young Charles' pony anyway, he was again humiliated by his wife coming to her defense. He thought of the girl running away into the forest. Once to escape his punishment for disobeying him. And then again, being defiant for who knows why. He damned his late wife for teaching Margaret to ride Night during their travels.

"Disobedient. And willful. Always disobedient. Not this time!" he promised himself.

"Margaret…Margaret," said Raymond even louder as he nudged his sister.

"Father wants you."

Margaret looked up and noticed the hall had filled with her father's retainers, villeins, and servants, even the kitchen staff. She pushed back her stool and stood tall. *The announcement!* She descended the dais and joined her father standing before it. She smiled at her father and gave him a deep curtsey.

"Some of you have heard the rumor my eldest is betrothed," Sir Charles began. "At Easter Court I met with Lord Edouard, Earl of Three Ridges. We arranged a marriage between his first-born and this girl."

Margaret's eyes sparked. She rose on tiptoe, calmed herself, and settled.

Sir Charles looked at the crowd, not at his happy daughter, who gazed at him with love in her bright eyes. From his sides he lifted both hands. They held documents. He raised his right hand high.

"This is my copy of the marriage contract." Then he raised his left hand. "This is Lord Ridges." Sir Charles paused for effect and glared at Margaret. "I regret to inform you that Lord Ridges has requested I nullify this contract. I have agreed."

Stunned, Margaret demanded, "WHY?"

The hall went silent and wary. Sir Charles' eyes narrowed. "I informed Lord Ridges of a rumor you had been with a man, that you had lain with a Saxon while I was at Court."

"That is a lie!" declared Margaret.

Caitlin's roar startled those in the hall. "That report is false! A damned lie! I have been with Margaret every hour since her birth. Whoever told you that rumor lied. I swear it! I will swear it before the church altar and to anyone who will listen to me!"

Sir Charles ignored her outcry and continued. "I asked him if he wanted you tested, if he still wanted the contract. He refused both offers and has returned his copy of the marriage contract. Worthless!" he announced as he threw both parchments into the fire pit.

Many gasped as they watched the documents smoke and ignite. His daughter saw her future burning and turned on her father. "Did you not defend me? Did you not inform Lord Ridges the rumor was a lie? I am a good girl, Father. In my whole life I have not even touched a man who is not you or Charles or Raymond. How could you believe such a story? How could you agree to my ruination? The rumor is false; I swear it!"

Sir Charles leaned and hissed at Margaret, "I know." He enjoyed her shock. Sir Charles stood upright and announced, "Your punishment is that you are no longer a part of my family."

Raymond's and Young Charles's jaws dropped. Cecily smirked.

Sir Charles grabbed Margaret's arm and turned her to the crowd. "She has disgraced me," he said. "I should throw her away and declare her a ditch woman."

Many gasped in horror.

Margaret frowned. *Ditch woman?* She shook her head in confusion. *Why is this happening?*

"When you laid with a Saxon you became a Saxon. You are a lady no longer. You may no longer bear a lady's name. From anon, you are 'Margery.' From this moment forward you will serve my family as chatelaine, sleep with the other servants, have no rank. EVER AGAIN!" he ended with a roar.

From the side doorway, Cook bellowed, "YOU have done this! Sent a falsehood to Lord Ridges. You have hated the girl's independence from your will for years. You do this to punish your dead wife for a bargain too dear. To have the dowry returned to you. You are ruining your own child for coin! We all know it!" came Cook's final accusation.

"SILENCE or I will have you BEHEADED!"

Cook did not move, did not speak. Arms akimbo, she glared at the man she had once respected.

Though her arm hurt from his hard grip on her, Margaret stiffened her spine and turned toward her father.

In a surprisingly serene voice, she said, "I am the Lady Margaret, your dau…"

With his free hand, Sir Charles slapped her face. "You are a slattern!"

"I am the Lady…"

Sir Charles struck his child with his fist and knocked her to the floor. He pulled her to her knees. No one dared stop him. She was his property to do with as he willed. Sir Charles released Margaret's arm, grabbed her braid and exposed her neck. As he drew his dagger from its sheath, two of his knights stood to stop him murdering his child. He pointed his dagger at them; they froze.

The foremost man said, "Dead she cannot serve you, my lord."

With a wicked sneer on his reddened face, Sir Charles sawed off Margaret's braid at her neck.

"NO, NO!" begged Margaret as she wept.

That he had nicked her skin and drawn blood pleased him.

Margaret fell forward, sobbing. Only her stiffened arms prevented her from falling onto the rushes. Sir Charles kicked her. Margaret fell to her side. He ignored the gasps. She drew her knees to her belly as her hands clutched at the ends of her chopped locks. Uncut hair had marked her a Norman lady of rank. Hurting too much to cry, she gasped for air.

"By law a Saxon's hair may not touch her shoulders." Sir Charles picked up the two-foot long braid and threw it atop the burnt parchments. He smirked as acrid smoke rose above the flames. "I make you my slave. You are Margery and…"

"Never! I am…"

The blows came hard and fast. He punched her head and kicked her belly. When she tried to rise, he socked her left eye and pounded her shoulders and back until she dropped her head to the ground and covered it with her arms. Her cries were fuel to his rage. No one dare stop him. He was the lord, all powerful. She was his property; he owned her. If he killed her, he would suffer no repercussions.

Senseless, Margaret lay in a heap in the dirt between the dais and the fire pit.

Caitlin stuffed her fist into her mouth to suppress her sobbing. Cook stepped back from the crowd and fled the hall. Many Saxons wept, and knights looked on in horror.

"Clear the hall! No one touches my slave. She gets up by herself or dies where she lies." Sir Charles bent over and hissed so only the girl could hear. "She is dead and can no longer defy and embarrass me. Now neither will you, slave. You will obey me or die as well." With that, Sir Charles waved his children from the dais and everyone from the hall. He glared at Caitlin until she turned away and fled with the others.

Hours later and only semi-conscious, Margaret lay still until she was sure she was alone in the now candle-less building, until the fire in the long pit was only embers. She moved slightly. Eventually she sat up, clutched a nearby bench and with much effort pulled herself to her feet. Still bent over, she looked about with one opt eye. *I dare not leave by their entrance. Caitlin. She and Cook will know what I should do.* The girl stumbled to the servants' door.

5

The Ghost

May

Norman and Saxon alike knew ghosts to be real. Ghosts had been real before Augustine had converted King Aethelberht to the Catholic faith in 597 A.D. Despite the church's teachings, they were still real and could stalk the living. Though many had listened to accounts and stories, none on Sir Charles's estate had seen one. This night the horror of a ghost visit became a terrifying reality.

Beaten so badly and so injured that she was insensible, Margaret lay in Cook's cubbyhole beside the kitchen. Cradling her charge in her arms, Caitlin froze when she heard a distant wail.

Through the blackness, guards on the palisade walkway looked toward the sound of pounding hooves approaching. Trying to espy what was coming through the trees from the south, the men leaned over the top of the poles. A half moon and a few stars peeked from murky clouds. A hooded figure wrapped in a pale mantle appeared.

It veered into profile on a horse so black it was invisible; the figure seemed to float. It swung west and started around the bailey just outside the tree line.

"The Devil!" cried out the gateman.

"Margaret! My Margaret!" it repeatedly screeched into the night air.

The guards ducked behind the palisade wall to keep from being killed by its look.

"Her ghost," whispered one guard. "Come to kill us for not protecting her daughter."

In the village, bailey, and barrack, those in their beds also heard the howling and pulled covers over their heads. They prayed to God and his saints to save their lives and keep their souls from being taken.

On the second level of the keep, Cecily cried out, "Father! Father! Save me!"

In their bed, Raymond and Young Charles clung together and whispered prayers to each other. Upstairs, Sir Charles was too afraid to answer his daughter, even to move.

The figure called out, "I know what you did! I know what you did!"

Again screeching, "Mar-gar-et! Mar-gar-et!" the figure completed the circle and melted into the forest.

Dawn broke before the priest was brave enough to rise, dress, and ring the bell for Mass. Only at that sound did anyone else on the estate move. Praying daylight had driven away the spirit, villeins cautiously lifted their blankets. Careful not even to glance toward the trees, villagers grouped together and tramped into the church. Knights who were supposed to have stood guard duty stepped outside the barracks into a day of gray clouds and a gray mist among the trees.

They approached the walkway and the men who had held their positions all night without relief. "Well?"

"Safe."

The men descended the ladders and strode to the chapel. Their replacements reluctantly took their places.

Despite not giving sermons on weekdays, Father Ambroise spoke a long time on God's love for his people, of His protection of the righteous, and of His forgiveness of sins properly confessed. No person dared look at another. The lord, his children, knights and Saxons filed out in silence.

Throughout day, every person was polite with each other. No one mentioned the long line outside the church of those waiting to have their confessions heard. By the end of the day, all in the village and those within the bailey had completed making their confessions. All except Sir Charles.

6

Refusal

May 10

Having been stripped of her Norman rank and clothing, Margaret stood before the dais with a blackened eye and in rumpled Saxon clothing and headgear. The hall was warm with a good fire in the pit, but no warmth pierced the girl's spirit. Margaret had covered her hair with a wimple to mask her forehead and head. It crossed under her chin, tied at her nape and hid her cut. She had worn it hoping this might prevent her lord from shaving her head, stripping her naked, and throwing her into the world. She stared at the floor with her arms at her sides and her fingers curled.

"Now will you be Margery and my Saxon chatelaine?"

Without looking up, Margaret shook her head. She heard his chair scrape against wood. Each hard boot stomp bespoke his fury. The first blow to her shoulder knocked her sideways. She remained standing. More enraged than ever, Sir Charles struck his daughter again and again. He ignored the grumbling of his men and saw not his sons looking away.

Margaret fell to the floor and curled into a ball to protect her insides. She lost consciousness after he kicked her in the head.

Again that night, the ghost appeared. Again, everyone trembled with fear and hid from the apparition. Again, they prayed hard.

Convinced the ghost was a hoax, Sir Charles demanded Margery be brought into the hall as soon as the phantom had disappeared. A knight walked in carrying the unconscious girl.

"Drop the baggage on the floor."

Instead, the man gently set her down and moved her head to a more comfortable position. Then he stood over the girl and gave his lord a hard look. He remained there until his lord warned him away.

A second knight dragged Jorgon by the nape of his neck before the dais Sir Charles was pacing. "Confess!" demanded Sir Charles. "You are playing the ghost. You hid that cursed animal someplace and wear your… former lady's… mantle and scarf."

Jorgon bowed and kept his head down. If his master knew the truth, he, his father and the girl would die.

"My lord, I know not what happened to the gelding Night after the Lady Rosamonde's death. It disappeared. I know nothing of your lady's garments."

Sir Charles left the dais and struck the boy. "Liar!" Sir Charles ordered the man who had brought Jorgon, "Pass a thick rope around that pole and attach this Saxon scum well. No food, no water until he confesses and produces that horse." Sir Charles struck again. Unconscious, Jorgon fell. His lord left for the keep.

Much later, Sir Charles's chatelaine and his hostler came awake at the same time. "My lady, move not. Pretend to be dead," whispered Jorgon.

Stirring, she asked, "What did he do to you?"

"Just struck me. I am all right."

Margaret tried to think what to do, but her jumbled brain would not cooperate. A knight came to the pair and addressed the girl. "You had best get away. Crawl if you must. I am sorry. I cannot help you." Then he whispered, "Caitlin is beyond the door."

7

Revelation

16 May

Margery stopped before the hut to which she had been summoned and inspected it. *Well-thatched roof, thick wattle and daub walls, usual doorway cover.*

Looking about the village, she decided she had best order work done on several other houses. Here and there, chinking had fallen. The woven withies, which were the interior of the mudded walls, showed. Rain would soften the daub further and soon a wall might fall.

She stepped through the doorway and dropped the oiled, cloth curtain behind her. *Table still damp from scrubbing. Dishes and pots on shelves. Smells clean. Well kept.* A glance about the single room confirmed her thought. *This family is more prosperous than most.* The couple's bed stood against a wall with its foot toward the fire pit that was offset from the center of the house. Bed covers were clean but worn. A tall, narrow wooden cupboard on the opposite wall held all their belongings, dishes and utensils above, and a few garments and bedding for their three children on the lower shelves. Next to the cupboard stood a wooden bucket half-filled with water. A pot and two pans sat next to the fire stones surrounding the few embers that had been kept burning. A table and stools took up the rest of the room. Margery stepped around the table and approached the sickened woman. She leaned over the bed and placed her hand on the woman's forehead.

"Goda, Aldrich said you have a fever, but I feel none."

When Goda started to sit up, her husband hissed, "Stay abed. Cough again."

Margaret frowned. The woman coughed, smiled, and lay back under the blanket. Aldrich moved his pointing finger to his lips to ask the girl for silence. He spoke loudly so Margaret's guard would also hear him, "Chatelaine, I am troubled. Please examine her carefully."

With that he picked up two stools and placed them beside the bed without causing a sound. He sat with his back to the doorway and pointed for Margaret to sit on the other stool. She sat and leaned over again to place her hand on Goda's forehead.

"Oh, my!" Margery started with great concern. "This is serious."

If the knight guarding outside the door had heard and looked in, he would have seen only backs and Margaret leaning forward.

Aldrich whispered, "We know your secret."

"What secret?" Margaret whispered back.

"Please know we almost did your mother a terrible wrong."

"What wrong?"

"We almost desecrated her grave, dug up her body to cut out her heart and beheaded her."

Margaret's jaw dropped. Then she closed her mouth and sucked in her lips. She took several breaths. "Why?" she demanded.

"We thought she was the ghost, that she had turned into one of the "undead." When a person dies strangely or too soon, sometimes the departed one does not leave this world. It stays on earth by sucking blood, ofttimes from the ones it loves. Animals and people sicken and die. When she called your name, we believed she was coming for you. We were going to dig up her body and perform the ritual to save you, dear lady."

Margaret envisioned what they might have done to her beloved mother and grimaced. *How dare they!* "You did that to my mother?"

"No, no. Jorgon Elder explained what his son was doing. At first we did not believe him. Men accompanied him into the forest. He showed us…" Aldrich looked behind him to be sure the knight was still outside. "You know what he showed us."

Margaret nodded. *The cave! He will kill Night if he finds him. God, keep Night safe. He is all I have that was Mother's.*

"We held a meeting and decided…"

Margaret interrupted him. "Who? What?"

"Village men I trust. To permit you to keep using the ghost. But we have conditions."

Margaret looked sideways at the man and then turned toward Goda, whose expression revealed she also knew Jorgon's secret.

"You only bring out the ghost when Lord Charles does something awful or permits something terrible to happen. The ghost stays out of the village."

"The dead go to God to be judged."

"No, child. We know sometimes they do not. Their spirits stay with their bodies; they walk the earth at night as the undead. Then they must be stopped."

"Who else knows?"

43

"Two other men, me and Goda; we needed her to get you here. Each has sworn to keep silent, reveal nothing, tell no one else. Not even in Confession. Act as if we tremble for our souls' safety like everyone else."

"Why are you helping us?"

"Because your mother…" Aldrich realized Margaret did not know what he did. "…loved you so much. If our silence over your deeds keeps your father" — at Margaret's scowl, the village elder changed his words — "keeps Lord Charles under some control, then we will be party to it."

"If any of you talk, Jorgon and I will die."

"Fear not, my dear. We are on your side. We do have a problem. If believers dig up your mother, they will desecrate her body. Mayhap publicly burn her heart to prove she cannot return." Margaret shuddered. "We seek your permission to save her from that. In the deepest dark, dig her up from the church graveyard and rebury her body in a secret place, so her body remains undisturbed further."

Margaret looked away. *Mother in unconsecrated ground? How can I allow that? Yet she must be whole for the second coming of the Christ. Mother, I must let them keep your body safe. Please forgive me. Oh, Mother, what else can I do?* After several moments she rasped, "In the forest." She added, "Please never reveal to me where."

Using water from the bucket and a pot placed near the embers, she began a weak tea of evening primrose. She whispered to the pair, "How can it be carried out in the dark? Burn a branch or light a candle and you will be seen."

"Supposed to be clear this night," he responded. "We will use the stars to guide us."

"Our guardian angels," Margaret said.

"Look down upon us, see and know everything."

"I will pray for all of you. Every night until I die," the girl vowed.

"Bless you, child," Aldrich added, "If anyone tries to dig up your mother's body, he will find a vacant grave. Proof the ghost is real. You will be safer this way."

As was usual and required, Margaret began with a prayer asking God to intercede; she prayed over each step, and prayed God would heal Goda so she would soon be well. She handed Goda the mug.

Speaking in a loud voice so the guard heard her, Margaret said, "I will look in on her on the morn after Mass. Aldrich, let us pray she is better." After they did so, the Saxon took Margaret to her escort and watched them depart for the bailey.

Mother, please forgive me. Look down from heaven and give me a sign I have done the right thing.

Late that night Margaret left the kitchen cubby despite Cook's sleepy warning.

"The Devil is out at night. Evils spirits too. You are putting yourself in considerable danger."

"I want see the holes in the floor of heaven while I pray. I am hoping my guardian angel is looking, guarding me."

As Margaret stood outside, all else was blackness; not even the buildings were visible. Above her were the only specks of light and a sliver of moon. *Please, God, protect them. Let them find a good place for her. Rest in peace, dear Mother. May God already have you in His loving arms.* In addition to praying for Cook, Caitlin, Jorgon, Jorgon Elder, Night, Aldrich, Goda, her brothers and sister, and so many more, she also prayed for her unknown benefactors. She continued a long time before turning back to her new abode inside the kitchen annex. Just before she stepped into the kitchen, she saw a thin shooting star dash across the sky and die. *Thank you, Mother. I love you forever.*

8

Acceptance

17 May

The next morn Cook moved from the kitchen hearth to face Margaret. Suffering another aching head, the girl had perched on a stool and leaned against the wall. She was black and blue on every exposed area but her palms. The edges of the original injuries were yellowing slightly, but not the new ones. Her broken ribs would not heal for weeks.

"One more beating and you will be dead."

"I am disgraced, a slave until I die. If he kills me, I cannot be condemned to Hell for all eternity. Being beaten to death is not suicide."

"Girl, have you lost your mind!" exclaimed Caitlin. "While you remain alive, you can hope."

"Hope?"

"God watches over you. Pray and be patient. He may astonish you."

"Hope for what? For freedom? A better life elsewhere? For him to die?"

"Choose one—or all three."

"Cook! Hold your tongue!"

Margaret smiled for the first time since her downfall.

Caitlin strode to her charge, set her hands on the sides of the girl's face and leaned forward. For as long as the girl could recall, this gesture meant her nurse was about to tell her something of great import.

Caitlin whispered, "Child, he is striving to kill you, and you are helping him. If he succeeds, you die and he wins. Do you really want him to win?"

Margaret frowned. *Do I?*

"Live and be a barb in his foot. His every footstep a constant reminder."

"Of what?" Margaret whispered back.

"Of his failures. To have justification to kill you. To destroy your spirit. Even to control you."

"But he does control me."

Caitlin shook her head; she pulled Margaret's forehead to hers.

"Only your body. Not your thoughts. Not your courage. Not your will to survive."

"He will keep pressing me until I fall or fail. Why tarry? Why not help hm?" the girl whispered back.

"Be not like him, an oak who breaks in a great wind. Be a willow. Let the wind move your branches, but not the trunk of you, the real you. When he realizes he cannot break your spirit and never will, he will tire of torturing you."

"Then what?"

"Then you know you have won. Live out your days, pray, and wait. He is already thirty-five, an old man, and he is drinking heavily. You are young and strong. Outlive him and be free."

Caitlin kissed Margaret's forehead and stepped away.

In deep thought, Margaret stared off. Caitlin worked bread dough as Cook stirred a pot and swung the blackened metal arm to return the stew over the fire. *Hope? For how long? Through what? Can I bear it? Do I even want to? Yes.* Suddenly, Margaret smiled.

"Where are you going?" asked Caitlin when she saw her charge stand.

"To save Jorgon."

"How?"

"I will grant Sir Charles what he wants—for a cost."

"Choose your words carefully. Your father is…"

"No longer my father. He is Sir Charles or my lord. Nothing more than that." She tried to inhale a deep breath, but her cracked ribs hurt too much. "I am no longer a child, Caitlin. He may call me Margery and keep me a slave and chatelaine to his estate, but I am still me." *I am not Margery. But I will obey his commands.*

Both women looked at her with awe.

"I request but one thing. Do not call me by that name. Address me as 'Girl' or 'You' or 'Chatelaine.' Will you ask the Saxons to do likewise?"

"Of course," said both women in unison.

"Thank you." The girl straightened her plain, brown garments and headscarf and then her back. With stately dignity she left the kitchen. Caitlin and Cook stared after her.

Margaret walked across the short distance between the buildings and stepped into the hall through the servants' door. The hall went still as the men watched her proceed forward and stand before the middle of the dais. They saw her bow her head, curtsey low, and remain there. She waited; they held their breaths.

I can do this. I must. Not just for me, but for Caitlin and Jorgon and Cook and the others. Still halfway to the floor, she uttered a respectful, "My lord."

He peered over his meal. "What do you want?"

"To serve you, my lord. As you have commanded."

"About time." Then he asked very loudly, "What is your name?"

"Margery, my lord."

Norman and Saxon alike breathed a sigh of relief—and of sorrow.

"With your permission, I am your chatelaine, serve you at your table and obey your commands. I will honor you and your family as a dutiful servant should." She gave no sign of hearing Cecily sniggering at her.

"I will test you, Margery."

Margaret stood and bobbed a short curtsey. "Yes, my lord."

She waited for him to speak. When he did not, she did. "As your chatelaine, I must relate a need."

"What now?"

"The stables lack one hostler, my lord. Your horses need tending by one they favor."

He bellowed, "You intend to save your lover Jorgon!"

Margaret hid her inner cringe at his false accusation. His first test. "Two of your horses are refusing to eat and are kicking at anyone who tries to approach them."

"Your lover is my food taster and lives or dies by it."

I need not poison him. He's drinking himself to death. I care not why. "I shall taste your food for you."

"Begone."

"Yes, my lord." Margaret finally looked up at the man before her. She added airily, "If you have need of me, I will be in the kitchen— cooking." She turned away to leave.

"Halt. Return. YOU will taste my food from whatever portion I choose. And sip every drink."

Waved away, she curtseyed before she exited through the servants' door. *A win for me.* Late that afternoon Margaret cooled herself at the kitchen half-door. She spotted Jorgon limping toward the animal barn. She hugged her midriff in happiness.

9

❖

Royal Trial

17 May

Meanwhile, in Winchester, King William sat secure upon his throne. He had already defeated and executed enough men to be cert he was feared and obeyed. One more would remind every man, great or small, they were safe not from his wroth. He carried the power to kill anyone who even spoke against him and this day he would use it. The magnificent Great Hall echoed with the murmurings of those who had been ordered to attend the trial. Seated on the dais at the far end of the giant stone building, the king wore his crown to exhibit his authority, but his lord chancellor conducted the proceedings. Like the rest of the court, Lord Bardoul knew this trial was only ceremony. Artus was already a dead man.

Two knights before and two behind escorted Lord Artus down the center aisle created by the members of the royal court and visitors, who had parted for the men to pass. They stood on both sides of the hall in small groups. The defendant stopped well before the dais. Lord Artus bowed. Facing the accused and the court, Lord Belleme and Lord Bardoul stood to the king's left. His chancellor stood to his right.

The chancellor unrolled a parchment and held it before him.

"Lord Artus, you stand indicted of treason, of speaking against His Majesty, King William the Second, and of plotting to overthrow his lawful rule. How say you to these charges?"

To the chancellor, he said, "I am not guilty. I am innocent of these accusations."

Then he spoke to his king. "Your Royal Highness, last month Lord Belleme invited Lord Bardoul and me to sup with him after Easter Court. While I was there, they conspired against you. When I heard their plans, I disavowed them and immediately left their company."

"On the contrary," replied the chancellor, "Lords Belleme and Bardoul swear it was you who plotted treason. At once, they proceeded to Court to report you. That you did not step forward before they did is proof of your guilt."

"That I did not speak is only proof of my fear of Lord Belleme. After all, I am his vassal. How dare I accuse one of such high rank of treason? He carries so much power and influence. Who would have believed me? I can do nothing about Bardoul's lies. He consorts with Belleme."

"What proofs have you of your innocence?" asked the chancellor.

"As we three were the only persons in the room, all I have are mine honorable name and mine sworn oath that I am speaking the truth. I give Your Highness my solemn oath I am your loyal subject who has done nothing wrong, who serves the Crown, and who honors your right to rule."

"Your report is no proof at all. Not good enough against that of Lord Belleme's, an baron of the realm who serves His Majesty with such zeal and loyalty."

Among those in the court, a group of three lords looked at each other with disbelief. They knew otherwise of the Earl of Shrewsbury and Shropshire. He had already cautiously begun seeking allies and had approached them. Everyone else shifted their stances in boredom. They were ready for this charade to end.

"I call for my right to trial by combat."

"Denied," said the chancellor. "His Royal Highness pronounces you guilty of treason. Your lands, goods, chattel, and fortune are forfeit to the Crown. In three days' time you will be beheaded. Let the priests prepare you."

Artus' shoulders slumped; he dropped his head and gripped his hands together. His stomach fell even as a sour bile rose to his mouth. He ordered himself not to faint. Then he righted himself and stiffened his spine—and his will.

"My family?"

"What of them?"

With hands extended palms up in supplication, Lord Artus faced the king.

"Your Royal Highness, my wife and children are wholly innocent. I beg you to be merciful to them and allow them their personal possessions and enough coin for them to reach my wife's family in Normandy."

At the king's short nod, the chancellor answered.

"Confess your guilt, and your lady and offspring may live and depart in safety."

Anguish and dread filled Lord Artus. To sacrifice his good name with a lie was almost more than he could bear. He shuddered. Then he chose. "I stand guilty as charged. I stand ready to die for my misdeeds."

"Your plea is granted."

King William cared not that Artus was innocent and spoke true of Belleme. William now knew his chief enemy.

Belleme thought he was still safe from the king. Lord Bardoul shifted his weight from one foot to the other. Members of the court saw Belleme's somber face. Only a few noted how his eyes had lit up. Most of the audience looked on impassively; all they wanted now was to dine.

"Your lady, your children and all their descendants are forever banished from England. Should any return, death be their penalty," declared the chancellor. "Remove the traitor from His Royal Highness's presence."

With much dignity, Lord Artus bowed to his king. The doomed man's guards escorted him from the hall. Those who looked upon Artus' stricken, shocked face pitied him.

The king looked to his left and decided to test the two men. "Belleme, Bardoul, I hunt in New Forest. Join me." William II, King of England, stepped off his dais and departed.

10

Taxes

29 September

By the end of summer, the girl now called "Chatelaine" had adapted to her new role. Because Margaret had been unconscious on May Day, she did not realize she had been forbidden to join any festal until the Midsummer celebration. She slept Midsummer night away while everyone else feasted and danced around a bonfire until daybreak. In the morning she expressed her gratitude to God for her first uninterrupted slumber in many weeks.

Margaret had believed her family was good to their Saxons until she lived among them and saw how her lord treated them. He made unreasonable demands and seized whatever he wanted. More than once he forced a maiden girl to his bed for a night and then sent her away in the morn. The villeins hated how he used their daughters, but they could do nothing. He countermanded the wardens of the harvest which made their work longer and harder than need be; he even dismissed Reeve's best advice. She saw worse when he was intoxicated.

More than once a week since Lord Charles had disgraced and disowned his daughter, he ordered Margaret to stand before the dais during a meal. Sir Charles then asked his sons, "How many sisters have you?"

Each time they avoided looking at Margaret and replied, "One."

"What became of the other?"

"Dead," the boys would say in unison.

Then Sir Charles asked his slave her name. She answered with a dip and the correct response. Only then was she dismissed or ordered to a duty.

Young Charles and Raymond avoided Margaret to the extent of even changing directions when they spotted her. When they summoned her, they did so calling her "Chatelaine." She appreciated their attempts at kindness and forgave them when they were forced to be cruel toward her.

On the other hand, Cecily hurt and harassed her. The girl commanded her sister do everything for her, or she demanded attention, especially when she thought her sister might be eating or resting. She ordered the slave empty her chamber pot. Once she even tripped Margaret as she removed it from her bedside. Margaret wanted to stumble and strew the smelly contents over Cecily but decided against it. *She wants me to react, lash out. Then she can have me beaten.*

"Thank you, my lady, for asking for me. I do so love serving you," crooned the family slave as she departed.

Cecily snorted in contempt and flopped on her bed in a snit. Later, she forced Margaret to watch as she rifled through her sister's marriage chest. Cecily took her sister's best bliaut and matching mantle, the necklace their mother had given Margaret, as well as the linens Margaret had hemmed and stored.

As Cecily dug through the chest, she muttered, "You and Mother. It was always you and Mother, never me. She barely acknowledged my existence."

Margaret's eyes widened at Cecily's words. *Are you punishing me for being left behind when Mother and I midwifed other ladies of rank?* Margaret stared off into the corner of the room, trying to remember a time when Cecily and their mother walked together, talked with each other. Other than a couple of times when Rosamonde was teaching Cecily stitchery, Margaret could not remember a time. *Mayhap she wanted Mother's attention as much as I longed for Father's. Mother's best clothes. Forgot I had them.*

Cecily delighted in taking both the blue and the green outfits that had been their mother's. She took almost everything. "Now Mother's things are mine. Margery, place all these things in mine own chest."

While Margaret did so, Cecily destroyed the rest of Margaret's garments by slashing them with her dagger and tossing the items into the fire on the first-floor fireplace of the Keep. Cecily ordered her sister's marriage chest carried to the center of the bailey and filled with wood. "Margery, set the chest ablaze and watch it burn to ashes."

Margaret pasted a tight smile on her face and stared into the flames. *These are objects. Only things. As chatelaine, I wear the scissors and the keys. Just as Mother did. I use her needle and thimble and even her sewing basket. They are what matter. If Cecily demands them, I will hand them to her and then sit. With no scissors or keys to the buttery or to the smoke house, I can do no work. One missed meal, and I will have Mother's things back.*

As the flames reduced the chest to hot embers, Margaret repeated her thoughts. She added fresh ones: memories of her journeys with her mother, their intimate conversations. She recalled the lessons she learned about the care of women lying in and how to aid them birthing their babes. Of being encouraged to love and ride Night. She remembered the first time her mother handed her a newborn to clean, the first time she let her hand the babe to its mother, the first time Mother stood back and let her lead as she and Caitlin delivered a babe. Margaret's smile became genuine. Lost in memories, Margaret missed Cecily's approach. She felt the sting of a kick in the shin.

"I hate you!"

"Yes, my lady. What else may I do for you, my lady?"

"Get out of my sight!"

Margaret bobbed a curtsey, turned, and smirked as she limped toward the kitchen. *She can only hurt me if I permit it. I am not to blame for Mother ignoring her. Am I?* As Margaret reached the kitchen door, Yolo appeared and nosed her hand. "Hello, boy," said the girl as she scratched his head. Sir Charles' favorite hunting dog whimpered and looked to the door. "Begging again, are you?"

Margaret sidled through half door as she pushed Yolo back. She stepped to the work table, reached under a cloth and pulled out a wad of bread dough. At the door she raised her hand as if to throw the dough far away. Yolo yelped and jumped. Margaret tossed the wad above his head and watched him leap. Yolo landed and swallowed the ball at the same time. Then he looked for more. "You are a pig! You will eat anything!" Margaret waved him away…"Begone"… and shut the top half of the door.

The second time the ghost had appeared, Sir Charles demanded Jorgon Elder sleep in the stables with his son. As ordered, they and Margaret appeared at the base of the keep. That they did so persuaded Sir Charles the ghost was his dead wife haunting him and watching over her daughter. He slowed his debasement of Margaret and even started avoiding her. He drank even more heavily.

That night the ghost again appeared and rounded the bailey. This time it hollered, "Cecily! Cecily! I saw what you did. Be good to her or I will take your soul!"

Cecily screamed in terror and peed herself and her bedding. Sir Charles ran to her and carried her upstairs to the safety of his room. He commanded Margaret and the Jorgons to clean her mess. Cecily cried so Sir Charles ordered her bed moved to his floor; she slept there for weeks. Sir Charles sent Jorgon Elder home and again ignored his stable boy. Before Sir Charles sought another bedmate, he forced Cecily to return to the second-level room.

Trying to find Night, Sir Charles led search parties into the forest to no avail. At first Margaret feared he would succeed in locating her beloved steed. When he did not, she wondered if a knight was helping Jorgon and Jorgon Elder hide the animal by riding Night for them. When the specter appeared again, and the three of them could be accounted for, she thought her relief. *Night is alive, safe. Friends, I have friends. Even with mother gone, I am cared for. Good people, Norman and Saxon. Now I know. Being one of them is not so bad. Better than dead. No longer pray he dies. Thank you, God, for being good to me. Caitlin is right. Leave him to you, Oh Lord. Your will in all things.* That night Margaret's heart ache eased and she slept soundly.

Saint Michaelmas Day, September 29, was tax day. Sir Charles's seneschal sat beside him at the table in the center of the bailey. Using the estate's accounts book, he informed his lord what each family owed. Besides their labors throughout year, they owed him twenty percent of their crops and increase of animals or the equivalent in coin. Because almost no villein earned coins for special labors or services they provided, they lived by the barter system. They either brought what was owed in animals and produce, or the seneschal recorded the duty owed in lieu of missing items. The next week, the Bishop of Worcestershire sent his tithe collector with his escort of a dozen warrior priests. The Church took its ten percent from everyone, including what Sir Charles's had added to his wealth from his Saxons. Two days later His Majesty's Shire Reeve arrived, also guarded, and took the Royal's ten percent of Sir Charles's original total wealth. While Sir Charles kept eighty percent, the Saxons had remaining only sixty percent of grain and animals to last them through winter and to the next harvest.

Margaret was busy feeding each group. In addition to their taxes of harvest, animals and the lord's coin, the estate owed food, drink and lodging to both parties of tax collectors. From Michaelmas forward, even his children avoided Sir Charles. He was never in a positive frame of mind after he paid taxes.

October was for finding stray pigs, gathering acorns in the forest for their winter feed, slaughtering and smoking meats, making soaps and simples, harvesting and drying late herbs, and more. In November, everyone gathered dead wood from the king's forest to keep their fires lit. From his own forest, Sir Charles ordered fallen trees harvested and fresh trees felled so they would dry and be ready for the next winter. By the end of the month, everyone from lord to the smallest villein was ready for Advent and winter.

11

Advent

3 - 24 December

During Advent, Christians increased their prayers, good works, donations to the Church, and alms to the poor. Because Jesus had not returned at the turn of the Millennium as anticipated, He was overdue. Believing the Christ would return on a significant date, many priests taught that He would judge the living and the dead on First Day, 1 January 1100. A century is but a moment to God.

In Winchester, the royal capital, more worldly individuals used Advent to prepare for Christmas Day, the king's twelve days of Christmas Court, and the Epiphany Feast Day of January 6. In anticipation of letting their homes to the king's guests, city dwellers scoured their houses, baked bread, and cooked for their guests. They doubled or trebled up living with other families, who then shared in the rents of the one or two available homes. Each day more families crowded together and made products to sell at the market days that began on December 26. The practical were more concerned with profit than prophecy.

On the Royal Oaks estate, Lord Charles' slave had secured the third point of her wimple behind the knot to keep her nape warmer. Despite the cold, the rains and harsh winds, Margaret's master had forbade her to wear a mantle. Caitlin had knitted her an undergarment using doubled, heavy woolen yarn. The low scooped neckline was unseen under the girl's shapeless brown gunna. The second shift stopped at her elbows and hung only to her knees. Margaret's mother's old shift protected her skin from its woolen scratchiness. She was warm in secret.

The day before Margaret's birth date, both Sir Charles and Cecily issued so many commands she ran from Mass to well past her usual bedtime. She fetched, carried, served, prepared special Advent dishes, tasted their food, and more. She could barely partake of a meal before they again summoned her.

On December 15 Margaret knew her birth date would be unannounced and uncelebrated. *Forgotten again. Oh well. Should be accustomed by now. Let it go.*

After Mass Sir Charles proclaimed, "My slave Margery will spend this day and night alone in church. No one will disturb her until we enter church on the morrow for our next Mass. She will use the time in prayer over her many misdeeds." He added, "Slave, do all I command."

Margaret curtseyed. Saxons cleared a path as she stepped to a back corner and placed her face into it. The building emptied in silence. After snuffing the altar candles, the priest also left. Margaret moved out of her corner and looked around. Covered with oiled skins, the four window slits did little to pierce the gloom. The lone candle on the stand beside the altar represented God's presence in His church and was the only light that remained. Without body heat to warm the room, Margaret soon saw her breaths. She clenched her hands together to keep her fingertips warm and walked in a large circle. *Standing behind the altar. Forbidden. Is it a sin? Do not care. Confess and perform the penance required for forgiveness.*

A brass chalice covered with a gold-embroidered cloth stood behind the brass crucifix in the center of the altar. Four tree stumps supported the long board upon which the holy items rested. Behind the altar in the priest's place, Margaret pulled the wooden chest from beneath the altar board and knelt on the cold, packed dirt. Margaret frowned. *No lock. Fear of committing a mortal sin keeps the contents safe.* Despite knowing she was alone, she glanced left and right before she opt the chest. Inside she saw flat parchments and spotted the edges of rolled ones. Careful to keep them in order, she picked up one document at a time, examined it, and stacked it beside her. Writing was foreign to her. *Only priests write the secret language of God.*

She knew not what she sought. Three rolled parchments covered the bottom. She remembered their positions before she removed the first one and unrolled it. She spotted a circle of wax with markings near the bottom of what she held so carefully. *Something royal?* She unrolled the rest of the document and examined the inking. She found letters that her mother had taught her when they were away from home. *Their marriage contract? The "C" of his name, the "R" of hers—just as she taught me. Are these our names below? Dates and numbers after them? What do they signify?*

She spotted the "M" word at the top of the list and touched the big letter with her fingertip. *Margaret? This is me!* With her finger she lightly traced her name again and again. She closed her eyes to commit it to memory. Without looking, she "wrote" it on her lap. She then traced it into the dirt beside the chest and wiped her finger on her gunna. After comparing the two, she smoothed out the dirt and tried again, this time examining each whorl and swirl as she worked. Holding the document away from her body, she stood and walked to the rear of the church. She knelt and retraced her name near the side wall. She carefully re-rolled the parchment and returned it to the chest. After replacing the other documents in reverse order so the first one was again on top, she pushed the closed chest to it place. She smoothed out the dirt she had disturbed behind the altar and walked back to her spot by the wall.

After kneeling she traced her name again and again, each time more deeply into the dirt and more deeply into her memory. Hours later she heard the main door latch lift. She smeared out the writing and leaned against the wall.

Sir Charles charged in and stopped short. He scowled at the girl on her knees. From his living quarters attached to the church, Father Ambroise opt the side door to the left of the altar. He walked past it, faced the cross and genuflected. The priest crossed himself before he turned around to his lord.

"Have you come to confess?"

"I have not."

"No Body and Blood of Christ for you. Begone from this holy place. You are out of communion with God and His Church." Glaring at Sir Charles, the estate priest crossed his arms over his chest and intoned Latin in a harsh voice. Sir Charles fled. Father Ambroise closed the main door.

"Father, you are stronger and braver than I thought. Is it permissible for me to pray for you? I do not want him to punish you."

Father Ambroise did not speak. Instead, he nodded, smiled, and made the sign of the cross above her head. He left the way he had come. Hours passed.

From the doorway left of the altar, a hand placed a slab with bread, cheese, and boiled vegetables inside the door. The hand disappeared and reappeared to deposit a mug of ale. That finished, the hand pulled the door shut.

Whose hand? Not the priest's. Big. Male. Norman or Saxon? Cannot tell.

Margaret knelt before her gift and prayed over her meal. *To You, Oh Lord, all praise and honor. Thank you for this food, this day, this friend. I am ever your servant. In all things I strive to do your will. Amen.*

She ate without touching the wooden board. She debated leaving the ale to avoid having to piss, but decided taking two sips would not create a need. She finished, stood, knocked on the door twice, and returned to her place. The plate and mug disappeared the same way they had arrived. Next, the hand deposited three blankets in a heap before shutting the door. She folded one blanket in half and spread it on the dirt floor. She lay upon it and rolled herself in the other two. Soon her body heat warmed her, and she drifted off to sleep. Before dawn, a cough behind the door awakened her. She rose, shook out the blankets and left them in a heap as if no one had touched them. The hand opt the door, took the blankets, and closed the door.

At the sound of the church's bells, Margaret stopped walking. Sir Charles found his slave still in the back corner with her face to the wall; he walked to his place in the first row. After Mass, Margaret was glad to remain until the church emptied. She finished her prayers of gratitude to God and for her unseen benefactor, schooled her face to a somber expression and departed.

12

❦

A Late Celebration

16 December

The next day "Chatelaine" shivered in the chilly wind and puffed little breaths through her nose as she exited the hall. Margaret dashed into the kitchen and banged the door behind her to hold in the warmth. The old woman greeted her with a cheery "God's good morrow to you!" without saying a title or her name. Cook fed the girl the same meal that was going to the dais. Then she followed the girl out of the kitchen to help her serve.

On the way back to the kitchen, Yolo approached Margaret. "Not this time," she admonished as she pushed him away. Yolo hung his head, and Margaret ignored him.

Later, many more than usual entered the kitchen. Knights came for a bowl of hot broth before or after guard duty. Cook smiled and asked Margaret to serve them.

"God's good morrow to you," each man said with a meaningful

pause and a smile as if he thought a name or title instead of saying one.

Despite the raw weather, during daylight hours almost every adult Saxon stopped by the kitchen or made the occasion to pass by her when she was in the bailey or village. Without nodding their heads or pretending to notice her passing, they whispered, "God's good morrow to you."

Sir Charles was his usual irascible self.

Instead of creating petty demands, Cecily ordered, "Margery, you will finish my Christmas Day outfit by the morrow."

"Yes, my lady," said Margaret as she curtseyed.

"I will inspect the stitches and know if anyone else but you sewed them. Every stitch will be yours or I will punish you."

"Yes, my lady."

Margaret kept her head lowered to hide her dislike of the wench. She repeated her curtsey and departed the hall. *Reconsider. She will never have the time I had with Mother. Poor thing. Just do as she asks. Forget her anger.*

After dark Margaret finally plopped on a stool before the kitchen fireplace and inhaled. *Broth in the pot. Flour and yeast. Grains soaking. Crackling logs. Golden glow.* Margaret extended her hands and feet to enjoy the heat and comfort of the place. Earlier she had hemmed Cecily's headscarf. Now Margaret set more wood on the fire for greater light. With the mantle bunched in her lap to prevent it touching the earthen floor, she rolled back the first arm hole and hemmed it. Margaret blew on her fingers to keep them limber. Unseen, Caitlin left the cubby where they slept, bent over her charge and kissed the top of her head.

"Have you enjoyed your day?"

The girl looked up and smiled.

"More than I can say. I matter to them. They still like me."

"No, my dear, they love you; their actions this day prove it. Even though the knights cannot protect you, they know you think them to be good. You tend to their illnesses, see to their injuries, and mend their clothes just as your mother did. The Saxons hear your regard for them in your tone. You have birthed three healthy babes. You make them simples and ointments for their aches and illnesses. He believes his orders are essential to the running of this estate because he has never recognized what both you now do and your dear mother did. Come to bed now. You squint your eyes and your shoulders droop. Finish that on the morrow."

"Caitlin, I dare not. I expect she will ask for it before Mass, and she will strike me if the mantle is unfinished."

"Do what you must. Afterwards, take to your bed and sleep through Mass. If Father asks why you missed the service, answer, 'Please ask Lady Cecily.'" This time Caitlin kissed Margaret on the cheek. Before she stepped into the tiny side room to sleep, she turned back to her former charge. "God's good rest to you, Child of My Heart." Caitlin added with a smirk, "Remain inside, no matter what you hear."

Margaret finished hemming the second arm hole as the first howl sounded. She delighted in hearing her name repeated.

Bless you for your gift, my friend.

13

Christmastide

25 December 1099 – 6 January 1100

From the king to the humblest slave, everyone in the realm cele-
brated the season the same way. Only the richness of decorations,
food and gifts varied. Every Saxon door frame displayed a sprig of
holly. Greens decorated every hall to remind the winter-weary that
spring was coming. Candles symbolized more daylight was returning; each day was a moment or two longer. Every Christian spent
Christmas Eve Day fasting consuming only water and confessing
their sins. Throughout the land, at midnight, church bells rang
twelve times. Every citizen entered his or her church to attend High
Mass and to receive Holy Communion. In this manner the whole
country became one body in Christ's church. On Christmas Day
everyone behaved decorously.

   After breaking their fasts, all but the cooks and servants went
to bed. The only meal of the day began at noon; the feast lasted

for hours. After sipping a first course of broth, everyone devoured as many courses as they could afford. After a month of meatless weeks, a roasted animal was the featured course. The royals dined on a variety of pork, venison, boar and exotic birds. Nobles ate pork and chicken; Saxons might have a chicken but were more likely to dine on rabbit or small birds. Honey, a rare treat that both reconstituted and sweetened dried fruits, appeared only on Easter, Christmas Day and Epiphany. At the royal table, dessert was a tower of sweetened fruits in the shape of an animal. Nobles enjoyed honeyed fruit in small, individual sweet cakes. If Saxons had honey to drizzle over boiled dried fruit, they were thrilled.

All afternoon people visited at table or in each other's homes. Adults not serving the ranked sat at leisure. Margaret was not one of them. Free from labor, youngsters played all day. After sundown the partying began. Tired children fell into bed. Now ale and wine flowed, and leftover foods held stomachs steady. Adults stayed awake to toast the First Day of Christmastide then to sleep until Mass. In country and town alike, the first late Mass began at eight in the morning.

The next eleven days were market days; towns saw countryfolk streaming in to gawk at the wealth of goods and to make purchases. Country folk did as little as possible with most hunting, resting, gaming, singing and having fun. For the ranked and the wealthy, ale and wine flowed and sumptuous meals punctuated each midday.

As his father had done, King William II held Open Court each morning from December 26 through January 5. The first day, every earl, baron, and lord of the realm appeared, gave obeisance, and recommitted his body and fortune to the service of the king. William Rufus demanded his brother Henry be first to do so. Afterward, any person in the realm could appear for redress or favor. The king began patient with the long lines, benevolent with his mercy, and generous with his gifts. Soon he tired of the duty, but he pressed on until time to sup. On December 27 he shortened the audience time from four hours to three. After the midday meal the king hunted with his favorites in tow. On December 29, the open court lasted only an hour. The king announced, "I am done! No more courts." William dismissed the line of supplicants and gambled away the day.

December 31 was the only solemn day during Christmastide. The fearful spent the day fasting and at prayer in church. The carefree continued partying until just before midnight. Then the less pious piled into church as well to await the coming year. When the Lord God and Jesus the Christ did not appear for the Second Coming, every priest in the land said a High Mass which included a stern sermon. "He could come at any moment. Every soul must stay prepared to meet its Maker and his Son," warned the priests. Afterward most people took to their beds. Others voiced their relief with, "Not this year! Who wants to return to talk, gambling, and keeping warm with more drink?"

Across the land the sermon on January 1 was similar. If the Lord God did not choose this day to return, remember the whole year is 1100. Best begin it in serious contemplation of Heaven and firm resolutions to prepare for it.

Despite the Church's best efforts, the morning of First Day re-started the entertainments. The holiday culminated on Epiphany with a second bacchanalian feast and the giving of gifts in honor of the Magi's presents to the Christ Child.

The next day King William dismissed the court. In the countryside, reeves began the tasks of assigning crop land for the year and of supervising farmers, who planted the pulses to be eaten during Lent.

14

Easter Sunday

8 April 1100

King William and his court spent the last days of Lent in Gloucester. After the Easter feast, the royal napped in his chambers. He woke and agreed to receive his visitor in his private audience chamber.

"Your Majesty, I come on behalf of God's Church."

"For three years one bishop or another has importuned me. I changed personal confessors and still I am asked what I will not give. When you address me as the Bishop of Hereford, Gerard, choose your words carefully."

The priest always weighed his words, whether in or out of court. "Archbishop Anselm seeks to return to England and requests your benevolent permission."

"You mean he has returned from Rome with the dead Urban II's order to excommunicate me. That new one, Pascal II, no doubt has given him the same charge. I will never admit Anselm into my realm."

"The Archbishop of Canterbury is God's highest representative in the realm. The Church and its bishops need his leadership."

"You are serving me well enough in leading God's bishops, Gerard. We have no need of Anselm."

Bishop Gerard well remembered King William's decree; no churchman leaving England could return. Lord Chancellor Gerard knew better than to challenge the king.

"As you will it, my king."

"Bishop Gerard, never ask this again."

"No, Your Majesty."

"Inform every bishop and priest the same."

"Yes, Your Majesty."

"Leave me."

Gerard obeyed.

Henry watched the prelate exit the king's wing. From the bishop's frown and slumped shoulders, Henry guessed his brother had again refused to comply with the Church's desires.

15

❧

New Forest

2 August

On a fine summer day of sunshine and gentle breezes below a cloudless sky, those attending the king into New Forest broke into groups and dispersed. Wanting to dine on boar the next day, William had ordered deer left alone. Hoping to gain favor, every man eagerly searched for signs. Because the beast was so dangerous, every man hunted on horse while carrying bows and arrows or boar spears.

Soon many heard a distant cry. As men stopped hunting, the news passed from group to group with a few men racing to inform others of the news. Men cried out to each hunting group, "The king is dead! The king is dead! A hunting mishap. The king is dead!" Nobles rushed through the forest toward the same spot.

The report soon reached the king's brother and his group of hunters. Frozen by the news, Henry stared at the messenger for a long moment. "I am for Winchester. Who is for me, follow!" he shouted. Without glancing backward to see who did so, Henry raced to the city.

Rumor and truth became so mixed no one was cert what had taken place. The king fell off his horse and a charging boar gored him with his huge tusks and killed him. He bled to death. The king turned his horse at the wrong moment, and a boar spear plunged through his heart and out his back. During the hunt, an unknown man pierced King William Rufus in the chest with a hunting arrow. The king was alone when someone in the forest murdered him.

By the time Henry had reached the hallway to the Royal Treasury to demand entry, the keeper had secured the realm's wealth and had hidden the keys. After arming himself with knives in his boots and his sword, the keeper guarded the treasury door.

Soon Henry and his followers stood before the sentinel. "It is I or civil war."

"Sir Robert is elder."

Henry shook his head. "You know Norman custom. The King chooses the next king from among his sons. My father passed over Robert for William. Well you know, he would choose me next over that wastrel." When the man did not move, did not speak, Henry added, "Robert is in the Holy Lands at the Grand Crusade. By the time he returns, our country will be torn apart with civil war; he will arrive too late to be king. Even if Robert could become king, my brother would spend every the coin behind that door within a year. Father passed over him for that very reason."

The Keeper of the Royal Treasury had heard of Robert's wastrel ways and wondered how to relent.

Henry knew he who held the treasury could gain the crown. Now was his chance, his turn to prove he was more his father's son than was Robert.

A party of the Earl of Warwick's men filled the hallway. Their leader reported, "We have secured the castle, Your Majesty. We are taking over the town."

The keeper admitted to himself, "He stands like a king, acts like a king, will be a better one than Robert. And no civil war." He gave Henry a tight nod. "I will fetch the keys, Your Royal Highness."

As Henry waited, he silently prayed for whoever had ended his long wait for the throne. Then he thought of his beloved Aegdyth. He imagined her reaction when she learned of William's death. She would be both appalled that a royal had died so violently and thrilled that Henry would have the crown he had so long desired.

Henry vowed to make her his wife and his queen as soon as possible.

Late that afternoon the reeve of Royal Oaks walked past the herb garden at the south end of the bailey and the woman on her knees. He turned his back to her and gazed across the yard. In a soft voice he reported, "King William died this morning. Hunting accident, they say. His brother Henry is in Winchester and controls the treasury. He claims the throne, and the Earl of Warwick supports him. Henry will meet with Saxon leaders and Norman lords in the morn because they fear a potential civil war."

Margaret nodded that she had heard but continued her work. Then she asked, "This morning?"

"Now you are one of us, I can tell you one of our sayings."

One of you? I am one of you!

"Saxon tongues are swifter than Norman hooves."

"Indeed they are if you know this the very same day."

Reeve smiled into the setting sun.

Henry's life may change, but mine will not. Mayhap never.

After Reeve departed, Margaret sank back on her heels and admired her neat rows of herbs and vegetables. She rose, picked up the basket of weeds and strode toward the pig troughs. *Saxon tongues are swifter than Norman hooves. Remember that.*

By twilight the next day most of the country had learned the news. Two days later a messenger arrived behind a royal banner with four knights escorting him.

"On Thursday, August 2, His Majesty, King William the Second, died in an accident while hunting boar. On the morrow in London, the Bishop of Hereford will crown Henry king. Henry de Beaumont, Earl of Warwick, will be at his side."

"No one fights Warwick," thought Lord Charles as he nodded acknowledgement of the news. "Send for Margery," he ordered. "My chatelaine will provide you housing for the night and provisions for the morrow. Please sit and take a mug of ale with me."

Sir Charles stopped worrying he would be summoned to take up arms. That Henry had taken charge pleased the Saxons; the one they favored had won. Many Normans liked that civil war had been averted, including Sir Charles. The men drank and talked among themselves as they awaited supper. Lord Charles remained on the dais and matched them mug for mug. That night he slipped into bed and a dreamless sleep.

In Shrewsbury and in a keep behind high stone walls, Robert de Belleme paced before a fire and cursed his misfortune. He had already smuggled some supplies into the country and was storing them in his castles at Tickhill and Arundel. He commanded some of the men he needed, but his men on the mainland were sending him mercenaries only by ones and twos. He possessed arms, horses, and all the provisions for a war to take the kingship, but he was hiding them on his estate at Ponthieu in Normandy. He downed another goblet of wine and threw the vessel across the room. It clattered against a wall and dented as it struck the stone floor.

"I shall not miss! After this harvest, I will finish my march to the throne. Henry will lose, and the crown will be mine. I swear it!"

16

Westminster Abbey, London

5 August

Two Henrys met before sunrise in a robing room in Westminster Abbey. A blaze in the massive fireplace had removed the chill from the stone structure. They sat in cushioned chairs at the corner of a long table carved with lion paws feet at the ends of stout legs. As no Christian ate or drank from midnight until after Mass, the table was empty.

"An auspicious day, Your Royal Highness," said Henry de Beaumont.

"I deeply appreciate your support, Lord Warwick. Is there anything you would like?"

"Peace. I want my properties to continue to be prosperous. I want my people alive and whole. Can you keep the peace?"

"Yes."

"Two brothers dying in hunting accidents. First Richard, now William Rufus. Bad business that."

"Indeed. And all too common. We both know that."

"Not certain about that Charter of Liberties. Giving Saxons back some of their former rights."

"I want their support. Without it, they may foment rebellion. What I have promised them will not affect any Norman privilege, right, or law."

"You also promised us redress of the grievances we had against your brother. What have you in mind?"

"After I am crowned, I will announce them at the banquet. No changes of rank or possession for any man who supports me. No increase of taxes for five years." Henry added with emphasis, "Unless there is war in the land or we are attacked from beyond our borders."

Warwick smiled at the royal "we" Henry was already using.

"Before you announce about the taxes, I suggest you remind them of the ten thousand marks your brother levied. Tell them you are different. You only tax for the common good, not personal gain."

Henry nodded agreement and continued, "I am considering awarding more royal lands to the barons."

"How much?"

"Ten percent more than they already possess."

"I suggest five percent — with no taxes on whatever they produce on the new land for that same five years. Reward our loyalty and then require we work for it."

"Good counsel, my lord."

"What of the seating at the feast? Who sits by rank down each table will be looked upon as signs."

"I will sit on the dais with two tables extended down the hall. That way each man will sit sideways to me and can see those on the dais. Would you like to sit beside me?"

Warwick shook his head.

Henry, soon to be King of England, knew Warwick's skills. Warwick's first contention to the Normans for Henry's kingship was that Robert was too far away and too weak of character. His second reason was Henry was strong enough to hold the realm together. Everyone already knew the earl had made Henry king. Warwick recognized no good would arise from sitting beside the new king. If the king failed, so would his own wealth and influence.

"The Bishop of Winchester is with you. Sit between him and the Bishop of London. A sign of the Church's support. It would also serve you well if you sent for Archbishop Anselm."

"Already done."

"I suggest you start with that announcement. Everyone will be grateful for his return. I propose four tables, each with a head man who decides whom to invite to sit with him and how many. One for the mayor of London will signal your support of our chief trading center. One for the priests; let Gerard, Bishop of Hereford, lead that one."

"One for you and the other barons," added Henry.

"Yes. And one for the earls and other dignitaries." Warwick added, "The Saxons still stand and serve." Henry nodded. "If you desire all this, I will see it done," offered Warwick.

"Thank you. I am ready for this Sunday this High Mass and then my coronation. Please inform the priests."

Warwick waited for Henry to rise first. The men shook hands. When next they met, they would be king and subject.

17

Convent of the Black Friars

27 October

In the chancel of the convent's church, the Council of Bishops watched Anselm, Archbishop of Canterbury, interview Aegdyth, Princess of Scotland. She was bareheaded instead of veiled. Her blond hair flowed freely to signal she was a virgin. Her bliaut of rich maroon with matching girdle and shoes contrasted well against the black and white of the bishops sitting on either side of the room. She stood between them, facing the Archbishop seated before her.

"My lady, yesterday you told us the story of your life and your education. Today we wish to hear more about your time at Romsey Abbey, near Southhampton."

Aegdyth looked at the stained glass windows above her. She admired the colored light streaming toward her and illuminating the chancel. She prayed for guidance to use the right words.

"I was sent to my Aunt Christina, who is Abbess there, to further my education. I have spent most of my life in a convent, but it was never to join but to shield me from…" Aegdyth blushed, "from unscrupulous attentions." She gave a tiny cough. "My aunt forced me to wear the white veil of a novice. I sought to wear not because I had no intention of becoming a nun. Once I stood before her, snatched it off, and threw it to the floor. I stomped on it. She beat me for that. Then she scolded me and explained the veil protected me from men. I consented to wear it in the presence of men or when outside the walls. I hope I am a religious person. I pray and follow the teachings of the Church. I try to do the will of God as He and others have shown it to me."

"Yet His Royal Highness said the first time he spotted you, you were bareheaded, as you are now. You were running in a field playing tag with other girls who were wearing the white veil."

"That is true, Your Grace. I had set it aside because of the heat. When he rode up and spoke to me, I ran to my veil and placed it on my head. He laughed at me and informed me he knew I was a maid, but not a novice."

"He reported that to us."

"Since then I have been permitted to see him twice a year while my aunt and other nuns supervise us. Your Grace, we have neither done nor said anything untoward. My aunt can give proofs of that."

"Will you place your right hand on the Bible and swear to God and to us that you never bore intentions to become a nun and that neither of your parents ever expressed a desire or plan for you to become one?"

"I can and I will."

"If the Church gives its consent, will you marry the king as he has asked?"

"Yes, Your Grace." Aegdyth's eyes sparkled with hope.

"He means to rename you Matilda, after his mother, because it is a more acceptable name to the Normans than your Saxon one. Do you consent to that?"

"Yes, Your Grace."

After Aegdyth swore as she had promised, the prelates dismissed her. She knelt beside her cot as she prayed hard and waited for news.

The following day, Archbishop Anselm visited her in the public room of the convent while the Abbess of the Black Nuns and two other sisters stood nearby. "Lady Aegdyth, the Council has decided you are not a novice and neither your parents nor you ever intended for you to become one." Anselm smiled his approval when she crossed herself, put her hands together in prayer and whispered, "Thank you, God, for showing me your will. I will obey."

Aegdyth kept her head bowed as she counted the years she had waited for Henry. How long she had prayed he become a king and still want her. Aegdyth's heart beat wildly at the thought of becoming Henry's wife. Over the years, marrying Henry had become even more important than her becoming a queen. Soon she would have both. She feared the Archbishop could hear her thoughts, so she quieted her mind and ordered her heart to slow. It almost did.

"His Royal Highness told the priest to announce your upcoming marriage at Mass this morn and wants you present to hear it. You will live here until you are married. You will wed in two weeks time on Sunday, the eleventh day of November. After the ceremony, he will crown you his queen with a celebration to follow. Does this meet with your approval?"

Aegdyth glowed. She forced herself to remain still, to keep her voice steady. "Yes, Your Grace."

"Sisters, please accompany the Princess Aegdyth as her chaperones. His Royal Highness has sent a guard of honor to take you to Westminster Abbey for the Mass and the first reading of the banns. You will return immediately." At the Abbess's nod, Archbishop Anselm led the women to the carriage the king had provided for them.

18

Royal Oaks, Worcestershire

9 February 1101

With the bailey already flooding in several places, the women were fortunate to sleep in the kitchen cubby's higher ground. In deep night, a sentry stepped into the kitchen; three heads popped from beneath heavy woolen blankets. He shook his fat-rubbed skin covering outside the door before shutting it.

"Chatelaine, he wants warm milk for his bedmate. Immediately."

Margaret rose as she said, "I will pour you a mug of hot broth. The cold and rain must chill your bones. Drink while I warm the milk."

"He requires it from the cow, and he demands you milk it and to bring it to him anon, I regret to tell you."

In Saxon, Cook growled, "He desires you soaked, cold, and sickened from this wet. An attempt to kill you."

The knight had spoken Norman. If he understood Saxon, he

gave no sign. "I will accompany you to the barn and escort you to the keep, my… Chatelaine."

Still a lady to him. "Thank you, Sir Bruis," replied Margaret with a smile.

After handing Bruis the mug, she touched the wick of a candle to an ember and encouraged it to life with a soft breath. She and the knight exchanged empty mug and candle. Margaret placed the mug on the mantle and reached for an oiled animal skin, her only protection against the wet. She followed Sir Bruis out the door. Lit torch in hand, Sir Ignace led the group. They stepped over the channel that directed rainwater from the kitchen toward the bailey wall and into the moat.

I am a duck. A duck paddling in pleasant, calm waters. When rain falls, it rolls off my back and enlarges my pond. I am a duck and I can paddle through anything.

"I am a duck," the girl murmured.

"What?"

"Nothing," said Margaret as she jumped another puddle.

All three shuddered as cold, damp wind swirled around them and attacked their oiled-skinned capes.

Sir Bruis pulled op the barn door and Margaret swept in. Careful to keep the candle lit, they shook their oiled skins only knee high. Bruis held the stub above his head.

Animals stirred and shifted in their stalls. They let the milkmaid know someone had entered the barn.

"Who goes there?"

"Margery and Sir Bruis," she answered as she took up a milk pail and stool.

"I will do that," offered the girl.

"Our lord wants me to do it. Back to your blanket with you. Dawn will arrive soon enough."

The girl pointed to a cow and said, "Change to that one, Chatelaine. She will give more milk."

Margaret did so and filled her pail. In the drenching rain, the trip to the keep was slippery and perilous. Bruis held her elbow as he assisted her up the stairs toward the keep. Holding a torch above his head, Sir Ignace stayed at the base of the ladder. After climbing the ladder to the entrance door, Bruis reached down and took the pail from her. Margery climbed one slippery rung at a time. At the doorway the knight pulled her onto the first floor. As he reached for the door, the wind caught it and slammed it shut.

A wench said, "Chatelaine, he is in a snit, pacing and yelling."

Still shaking the rain off the slick skin that had covered her from head to waist, Margaret answered, "I thank you for the warning." She picked up the pail and carried it up the stairs to the floor which had been her mother's. She knocked on the door.

"My lord, I am here to serve you." *I am a duck. Rain and words roll off my back.*

"Enter. What is that?" Sir Charles demanded as he pointed to the pail.

"What you ordered. Fresh from the cow I milked myself."

"I made no such request. Take it away. I wanted it after Mass. Not now. Do it again and bring it me then."

Margaret heard giggling coming from under the bed covers.

"My lord."

"After Mass and before I break my fast, slave."

"Yes, my lord."

More giggling.

95

When she stared at his feet and refused to look at the room, newly decorated, or at the bed chamber with its curtains closed and newly filled, Sir Charles tired of his latest game.

"You have my permission to have your Saxon lover warm you this night. Begone."

"As you order, my lord." *As if he has not hurled that insult before!* With her eyes still on the floor, she backed out of the room and closed the door. *I am a duck.* At the base of the stairs, she placed the pail by the servants, who lay abed rolled in their blankets as close to the fireplace as they dared.

"I am mistaken. He desires this treat for you. Please enjoy this milk and return the pail to the barn on your way to Mass. I pray God give you a good rest." She ignored their thanks and farewells. She spoke nothing to Sir Bruis as he helped her down the ladder or to Ignace lighting their path down the hill until she was at the kitchen door.

"I thank you, Sir Bruis, Sir Ignace, for your services. I ask God to give you a safe walk to the barracks and a good rest."

In the kitchen, both Cook and Caitlin awaited her. They stripped her of her soaked gunna, knitted tunic and shift, swathed her in a warmed blanket, set her on a stool, and replaced her soaked socks with warmed new ones. Margaret pushed her half-frozen feet toward the fireplace embers. In a monotone she reported all that she had done as she sipped hot broth.

"I knew it!" exclaimed Cook.

"If he wants you sick, then take to your mattress and be sick. Three days ought to do it."

"Do what, Caitlin?"

"Cause him to appreciate you. We will offer to taste his food. To him we will send every Norman and Saxon for an answer to a question or for a solution to every problem. You stay abed too ill to speak. Cough if anyone enters."

"I could use the rest. He will punish me afterward."

"If he does, then relapse," offered Cook. "Two days more should do it. Then rise and be well and cheerful. When he accuses you of lying, thank him for his concern."

Be a duck. Let it roll off my back. Margaret shrugged. She coughed and smiled. Then she sneezed for real.

"That does it!" exclaimed Cook. "To bed, you poor sickly thing."

Caitlin and Cook bundled her into another warmed woolen blanket and placed her on her straw mattress in a corner of the cubby attached to the kitchen.

"The warmth in this room should help you. Ignore the bell for Mass. Sleep all day. You require it more than you know," advised Caitlin.

As she tucked the blankets around the girl, she heard a soft "Duck who can sleep."

"What said you?"

"Nothing," she murmured.

Caitlin rubbed Margaret's back as she dropped into a deep slumber.

19

Loss

March

"Does she live?"

The woman nodded. "Still sickly, Your Royal Highness."

"Show it me."

Careful of what she held, the midwife curtseyed. "I cleaned him as best I could, Your Royal Highness."

Henry nodded. The woman extended her hand and reluctantly undid the top wrapping. The one underneath was a little moist. She removed the inner cloth.

Henry swallowed hard. He steadied his stomach by sheer dint of will. "So tiny," he whispered.

No one spoke.

"Why are his nails dark?"

"I know not," admitted the midwife with a small head dip, "Your Royal Highness."

"Was he breathing?"

"Her Royal Highness said she never felt him move."

At the king's nod, she carefully re-wrapped the figure. Not knowing what else to do, she held the tiny bundle with two hands.

Henry turned to William Giffard, Bishop of Winchester.

"He would have been my heir apparent. I require him buried in holy ground."

"My son, he had not yet been given his soul."

Henry glared at the prelate.

"A proper grave. And marked."

Bishop Giffard bowed his head and said, "Yes, Your Royal Highness. I will see it done myself. And have Masses said."

"Thank you, Your Grace."

With both hands, the midwife extended the babe. With both hands, the bishop took it and held it to his breast. He nodded to the king; Henry nodded back and looked away. Not even the rushes on the castle floor sounded as the bishop departed.

"I will go to her."

The midwife curtseyed. "With your permission, I will look in on her."

Henry followed her through the audience, sitting and sun-rooms but stopped short of the door to the queen's inner chambers. Carrying various items and a basket of used towels and clothing, several women filed out the doorway. They gave obeisance as they passed the king, who was looking out a window slit at the rain and saw them not. Henry inhaled a deep breath and stepped through the opt doorway. The Lady Claire de Clerkx and two other women of rank curtseyed.

"Leave us. All the way out of this wing. Shut every door."

Henry pinched dead all but two large candles on pedestals near the doorway. In the dark end of the room, he sat on the edge of Matilda's bed and stroked her loosed hair.

"You are so pale, my love."

Matilda's tears flowed as she choked out sobs.

"I am sorry. So sorry. I felt sick. I could not keep him inside. I lost him, Henry. I lost him."

"Next time, my beloved, next time."

Henry lay beside his wife and drew her into his arms as she continued to weep. He gulped hard because he could not bear to see her in such pain. Henry was grateful that Matilda had laid her head on his chest. She would not see his eyes fill and spill over. Together they mourned for what might have been.

20

Murder

April

On the top floor of the keep, Caitlin knelt beside the corpse; Margaret waited in the doorway.

"Still warm."

"This was Mother's chamber," whispered Margaret.

"He probably pushed Fearn to the floor so she would not die in his bed."

"Did he strangle her?"

Caitlin shook her head and pointed to the rushes.

"You need to see this."

Margaret stepped gingerly. She smelled the vomit before she caught sight of it and gagged. Turning away and stared at a wall until she quelled her roiling stomach. "She stinks like Mother did."

"We understand why. Do you recall what your mother accused him of?"

Stunned, Margaret turned to face Caitlin. Her legs collapsed and she fell to her knees. "He poisoned them both! Why?"

"Fearn was with child. Insisted he marry her and make her a lady. She would not accept his refusal."

Margaret's eyes narrowed; her tone hardened. "Mother died because of me. The marriage contract. The dowry. My fault she is dead."

Margaret rose to flee. Caitlin caught her in the doorway. As she shut the door with one hand, Caitlin held Margaret with the other to prevent her leaving. "If he suspects either of us knows, he will kill us both. I do not want to die."

"I killed Mother!"

"No. No. They had fought for years. I think he got the poison in Gloucester. Wanted to use it there. She slept in the women's wing. Ate where the king sat her. He did not have the chance." Caitlin hugged her charge close and whispered, "We must find it and destroy it, dear child. Before he uses it on us."

Margaret's breathing quieted. She offered, "He would keep it close. In this room."

The women stared at clothes in piles, boots and slippers left here and there and dirty dishes on tables.

"He did command us to 'clean up the mess.' I will begin with the bed. You start with the room," ordered Caitlin.

Margaret shuddered. She set the mugs beside the closed door, added the chamber pot and dishes. She piled the girl's garments by the door and placed his clothes on the wall pegs. *Mother hung her clothes here. He killed her. I vow he will suffer.* Margaret's stomach roiled again at the thought of the deaths.

Caitlin had punched the canopy from below, but nothing was on it. She inspected all the parts of the bedding before she straightened them. She crawled under the bed and felt nothing in the rushes.

"Nothing here."

"Nor in his pockets. He could have it with him."

"No, he is a coward. Afraid its nearness would sicken him."

Margaret leaned against a wall and raised her eyes to the Lord in silent prayer. *Please God. Show us where it is so he cannot poison anyone else. I promise to be good. I promise to obey your will.* As she gazed at the ceiling, over the bed she spotted a corner of wood a different color from the beam. She pointed.

"Found it!"

Caitlin joined her and looked where she was pointing.

"Good girl! Bet that is a wooden box. I am taller than you; fetch me a stool."

Caitlin knocked the box from the timber and onto the bed canopy. She held a bed post as she reached for it.

Margaret handed up a rag.

"Use this. Don't touch it."

Caitlin stepped to the floor. She opt the box and saw a small pouch with a drawstring pulled tight. It smelled of something dry, harsh, bitter.

"Do you recognize it?"

"No."

"What do we do with it?"

"Fetch my box of herbs and a clean rag to wrap this stuff in. We dare not replace the sack, but we can try to duplicate the look of the herbs. The odor of the sack should be sufficient to convince him if he checks the box."

"What if he uses it again?"

"We pray the stuff on the sack cloth only taints the clean herbs. Just sicken a victim."

Once they had completed the transfer, Margaret returned to the wall and directed Caitlin, who placed the box so it was again in its original spot with just a corner showing.

Margaret covered her face with her hands. *Cry not. Crying will reveal our secret.*

"Send for three men to carry Fearn to her family. Two more must shovel away the soiled rushes; wenches will remove the mess at the door and empty the slop pail," instructed Caitlin.

By the time Sir Charles had returned from the hunt, Fearn's body lay her parents' home and was already shrouded. Father Ambriose attended the mourning family. Villeins prepared for Fearn's funeral. Sir Charles rode into the bailey without even glancing toward the crying coming from the village. Margaret met Sir Charles and his sons in the yard.

"Is my room clean?"

Sir Charles' chatelaine curtseyed and kept her eyes down. "Yes, my lord, with the rushes repaired and scented. A pitcher of ale awaits you."

Sir Charles dismounted and threw his reins at Jorgon. Young Charles and Raymond dismounted and handed their reins to the boy before following their father to the keep. The dogs followed the servants carrying the game to the slaughtering table.

He went hunting as Mother lay dying. Did not return until she was dead. Margaret sucked in her lips and gave Jorgon a sideways glance.

No one saw him give a slow blink of agreement before he led the horses to the stable.

That night the ghost circled the bailey as it shouted, "I know what you did! I know what you did!"

Sir Charles got drunk.

The next day the villeins buried Fearn.

That night the ghost shouted again and again, "They both are in heaven. Hell is waiting for you!"

Sir Charles drank himself into oblivion.

Normans and Saxons alike knew why the girl had been murdered and who had killed their beloved Lady Rosamonde. Because they had no power to punish Sir Charles, they shunned him, looked only at his knees or feet when he addressed them, and kept well back of him at church.

Margaret continued to carry out her lord's commands, but her thoughts turned from survival to revenge. Even during Mass. *You need justice, you drunken old man. Kill him? I die too; Charles is not yet of the age to rule the estate. No murder for murder. What if I am wrong? We both are? Is it poison in that box? Something else? How to test?* Outside the church door she felt her hand being nudged. She looked down at Yolo. *Just a pinch inside a hunk of meat to be sure. I know you will gag and toss the meat. Then I can tell Caitlin.*

Margaret petted the hound as she led him across the bailey. Yolo wagged his tail in expectation of a treat. Margaret reappeared from the kitchen holding together her thumb and pointing finger. She held the tainted morsel away from Yolo, who sniffed toward her hand as she led him between the lean-to of wood and the palisade wall.

On the third night, the ghost repeatedly shouted again and again, "Confess or get you to Hell!"

The next day everyone waited for their lord to awaken and become somewhat sober before his first-born son dared give his father the news. Yolo had been found dead with foam around his muzzle. Sir Charles stumbled to the place and looked upon his old friend. He leaned against the palisade wall and vomited. No one suspected poison. Everyone assumed the ghost had killed the animal. A servant picked up Yolo's body with a wooden shovel and tossed it into the moat.

From a distance Margaret looked on, stricken by her actions. *What have I done? I am so sorry, Yolo. I just meant to test the herbs to see if he killed my mother with this powder. I only wanted to punish him for poisoning Mother. I only meant to sicken you to prove these were the herbs that did it. I didn't mean to kill you—just to see if a pinch would sicken you. Would that you had gagged and tossed the meat. That would have been proof enough for me and you would still be here.*

Margaret forced herself to keep a straight face and act impassive. Saddened, she turned away from servant's work, hid behind a grain bin for a time, and came out with swollen eyes. *Now I must live with my mistake and foolish pride. And confess my sin. Do penance for wanting to hurt him by sickening his dog.* Margaret avoided looking into the moat on her way to the church and Confession with Father Ambroise.

Two days later a sober Sir Charles spent all day with Father Ambroise. From that time, Sir Charles stayed in the church after Mass. He ate only the noon meal and drank but one mug of ale. After a month and a day of abstinence and good behavior, Sir Charles took Holy Communion at Mass and joined the hall to sup. Each day he continued to pray all morning.

Margaret carried on as before, but she remained unconvinced of her lord's improved behavior. *You are better now, but I do not believe your change will last three months. I can hope. For all our sakes I shall pray it will last.*

Ten days later, an anonymous person pushed over a lit brazier in the keep. When the rushes on the top floor flared and the roof flamed, servants ran inside. They picked up what they could to toss out the main door before dropping out the doorway or using the ladder to escape. The entire wooden structure blazed in the sunshine. A pail brigade from the nearest well failed to save the structure.

Sir Charles and his sons returned from the hunt. They found Cecily hysterically crying and a pile of smoking ashes. No one saw who had caused the accident; the household servants appeared shaken and contrite. Sir Charles and his children moved to the platform above the storage rooms at the rear of the Hall. Having lost heir bedding, the family slept on mattresses and blankets taken from the Saxons.

Margaret sent out word to the sentries to linger near the road and urge anyone passing by to inform peddlers Sir Charles required bedding and other household supplies destroyed in the fire. That night Margaret sewed new bedding with ticking from a storage room. On the morrow, Saxons would filled them with straw.

The Saxons smiled themselves to sleep. Fearn's murder had been avenged.

21

Margaret's Ride

20 June

Jorgon Elder held Margaret's hand as he moved through the trees in the warm summer night. He was fast of foot even as only a sliver of moon illuminated their way.

"Sober only a month, now he drank himself senseless. Getting away was simple," she explained. *I did nothing; his fall is his own doing.*

"How did you go out, Girl?"

"Someone — I cannot tell you who — opt the gate for me. He will wait for me until I return."

"We heard a commotion in the bailey. A knight summoned Father Ambroise."

Jorgon Elder hoped relating what he had heard would loosen her tongue. He turned and led her further into the woods. They weaved in and out of faint light.

"Displeased with the butter, L-o-o-rd Charles came to the kitchen looking for me, but I was working in the keep. He charged into the barn and beat the milkmaid. Someone fetched Father Ambroise while a knight pulled him off the girl. When I reached the yard, Father was hollering at Sir Charles about being drunk and having to start anew. Sir Charles swore at him and yelled back, 'Not until the morrow!' Then he stormed back into the hall. Everyone disappeared. The knights supped in the barracks. His sons found Sir Charles drunk with his head on the table. His children supped in the kitchen."

In the distance, Night whinnied. "I am coming!" Margaret cried out as she ran up the path ahead of Jorgon Elder. Night's whinnying was even more shrill.

"Keep him bound until he calms," called Jorgon's father from behind her.

Margaret was too excited to hear him.

"Night! Night! Oh my precious Night!" exclaimed the girl as she stepped into the cave. She reached out to her horse as he pulled at the ropes to extend his nose to her. Night blew at her as she grasped him and kissed his forehead again and again. She stroked his cheeks and neck while softly speaking words of affection and praise.

"You are so patient, my boy. I have not seen you in so many months! I have yearned for you so. No one has missed you more than I. And you have done well in staying hidden. You are so good. Thank you for accepting other riders. You must have been desperate to run if you let them ride you. You must stay hidden, but I will ride you tonight," she said as she stroked his shoulder.

Night snorted as if he understood her.

"You always sense what I am thinking, boy. Yes, you do!" She hugged and stroked Night's neck. "I love you so!" she blurted as

Night snorted approval of her hugs. "Jorgon Elder, I want to saddle him. I want to do everything."

"Yes, my lady."

The man pulled his forelock as he lowered his head. Pleased at his words and action, Margaret stepped away from Night and hugged him too.

"You will always be 'my lady' to me," he muttered above her head.

Margaret hugged him again. "Thank you. Thank you for everything you have risked for me. For Night."

Night snorted in protest and stomped a forefoot. Back she flew. Jorgon Elder brought the saddle blanket, side-saddle, and bridle to his mistress. Finished equipping her beloved horse, Margaret stepped around Night's head to see that Jorgon Elder was holding her old container of sand. More lay against the cave wall.

Three other riders? Jorgon, Jorgon Elder, and who else?

The old man hung the sack on the back of the side-saddle which was overloaded and tipping. He grabbed saddle and sack to straighten them. Jorgon Elder offered a cupped hand. Margaret put a foot in it and bounced into the saddle seat. As Margaret tilted back dangerously, he grabbed her ankles to keep her and the saddle from sliding backward.

"You have lost weight, my lady. You are too thin. Grab his mane to steady yourself. Lean well forward while I lighten the counterweight." Jorgon Elder pulled several handfuls of sand from the sack. "Sit up but still cling to his mane," instructed Jorgon's father. "Now wriggle in your seat to see if the balance is correct." Jorgon Elder returned half a hand of sand before tying up the bag.

"Steady, boy," said the old man as he patted the prancing gelding. Jorgon Elder kept a quieting palm on the horse's withers as he rounded the animal and faced his lady. He noted that Margaret had already kicked down the foot platform and had set her feet upon on it. She was ready to ride. Night's head was still roped to rings pounded into both sides of the cave wall, but his backside bounced side to side. He neighed his eagerness.

Jorgon Elder handed her a strip of pale cloth with a slit in it. "This is for your forehead and between your nose and mouth, so your face looks like a ghost's."

After Margaret had fastened it behind her head, the old man handed her a triangle for her chin and neck. He passed up the pale blue head scarf, which she sniffed in hopes it still smelled of her mother. It did not. Margaret sighed. *I still miss you. I will always miss you.* He gave her the matching mantle and watched as she wrapped it around herself. Because Rosamonde had been taller than her daughter, even the girl's feet were covered. Margaret was all cloth except for her eyes.

"Will I look blue?"

"Moonlight fades it. No one has noticed or commented on it thus far. What will you yell?"

"Do not beat the Saxons?"

Margaret quieted Night with pats on his neck. She whispered something to him.

"When Lord Charles tried to stand, he fell and bashed his chin on the table. Knocked himself senseless and fell to the dais floor. That will bruise. When he awoke and struggled to rise, he bumped the back of his head against the underside of the table. He misstepped off the dais, took a tumble and collapsed into the rushes. He will be sore from that too. A servant tried to rouse him by tapping him. When he did not stir, the man pinched him and struck his shoulder hard several times. Still, he did not stir. Later his sons found him uncon-scious, whether from drink or his fall, I am not cert. They covered him and left him in the rushes. Now he is alone in the hall. On the morrow he will be black and blue — and very sore," said the elder Jorgon as he chuckled. He gazed at Margaret. "Why not yell, 'Beat a Saxon and I beat you.' He will believe it. That the ghost was within the bailey will terrify him. Mayhap he will beat no more Saxons."

"I knew not of his falling. You heard all that occurred even before I told you!"

Jorgon Elder shrugged. His eyes twinkled in the darkness when he saw his lady's smile.

"'Saxon tongues are swifter than Norman hooves,'" she quoted. "Even faster than Night's."

Jorgon Elder patted her boot. "He will believe if you yell, 'Beat a Saxon and I beat you!'"

"I could kiss you for that!" Margaret exclaimed. "So be it. I will shout that. How shall I return?"

"Night knows the way. Just do not allow him bash you with tree branches. I will await your return."

Margaret leaned until her chin touched her gelding's neck while the old man removed the ropes that tied horse's head to the rings. Night flew out of the cave and wove through the trees.

22

❧

A Plan

22 June 1101

After freeing Matilda's attendants, Henry watched the queen's ladies close the bedchamber door behind themselves. The royal pair sat upon comfortable, cushioned chairs in the solar with the afternoon sun streaming into the room.

"I found her, my dear one. The best midwife."

"Who?"

Henry stroked his wife's hand.

"Norman. Famous for delivering healthy babes. The lady lives northeast of Gloucester in Worcestershire." Henry moved nearer as he continued whispering. "I will say no name. Who knows what someone may overhear."

Matilda nodded.

"I am fetching her to make her one of your ladies. Our next son will be healthy and born alive, I promise."

"Only God Almighty can promise that."

"You pray to God while I fetch help." Henry paused and asked, "Two months and no one suspects? No one has even asked?"

Matilda smiled and shook her head.

"A Saxon servant is secretly helping me. Last month and this she wore my linen rags and bloodied them for me; I put them on and cried. My ladies have already passed the news; they are unaware."

"Good thinking, my dearest. Keep doing that until we can no longer deny it. Better that way."

"When?"

"I depart at dawn. Make stops there and back. Both for need and to hide the obvious. I will inform her lord I want his counsel for a considerable time and instruct him to bring his lady to keep him company. He will escort her. After I send a message of his coming, please prepare a chamber for them. I will make stops on my return and arrive two or three days after they do. Their arrival will arouse only curiosity, not suspicion."

"We are in agreement. Other than this lady, only we know until he comes alive and kicks me."

"You must not appear worried, my love." Henry touched her brow and drew his finger down her cheek. "We will nap and rest you. Let them believe we are still trying to conceive."

Matilda looked askance at her husband.

"I will not endanger him," promised Henry as he grinned at his wife.

"And I will not permit you to do so," responded Matilda as she smiled back.

Author's Note

My portrayal of King William II of England is historically accurate as to his taxes, his policies, and his requirement that barons and earls appear at three courts each year. King William died in New Forest on August 5, 1100 C.E. Nowhere in my research have I found historians in agreement as to the manner of or at whose hand the king died, though William Tyrel is usually mentioned. Only after William's death did accusations of sodomy begin to circulate.

Three factions did not want Henry to be king: his brother Robert, several barons and earls with lands in both England and Normandy, and the Church.

During this time, rumors circulated that Robert de Belleme desired the crown. King Henry's brother, Robert, Duke of Normandy, invaded England on July 20, 1101, to gain the throne; Belleme and others had joined Robert. After Henry stopped the invasion, he built a case against Belleme of over 40 charges of breaking the law, found him guilty of treason, and chased him all over England in an effort to bring him to justice.

From 600 to about 1200 C.E., the Saxons firmly believed in and feared the "walking undead." When individuals or animals sickened or died for unknown reasons, Saxons believed they saw the "undead" and blamed them. As a remedy, a recently dead person's body was exhumed. The person's heart was cut out to be burned before witnesses. The body was beheaded and then re-buried with its head laid between its feet to stop it from harming the living.

Lady Margaret represents noblewomen's circumstances in the early 12th century. Girls were the property of their fathers, who had the power of life and death over them. Marriage was a three-step process. Between five and twelve years old, a daughter was contractually betrothed. Once betrothed, the girl was sent to her future husband's home to learn from his mother how to run the estate and become its chatelaine. As soon as her courses (menstruation) started, the couple appeared at their church for the Church's blessing of the union, and the marriage union was consummated. She was then her husband's property. Many girls were mothers by thirteen or fourteen. Dying in childbirth was a common event for all women, even the highly ranked. The average life span for both men and women was about forty.

For six years, King Henry had waited to wed Aegdyth. After Henry's coronation, he set about marrying her and making her his queen. In London, Aegdyth appeared before Archbishop Anselm and other bishops during their inquiry as to whether or not her parents had intended her to become a nun. The princess's explanation of why she was beaten at Romsey is historically correct, as was the reason for her name change.

Some historians wrote Queen Matilda miscarried a son in March 1101. When I learned that, I asked myself three questions: What if her miscarriage were no accident? What if she had been poisoned to prevent King Henry from having an heir? Who might have done such a thing? The books subtitled "Henry's Spare Queen Trilogy" are my answers.

Excerpt

Lady Margaret's Escape
Henry's Spare Queen Trilogy Book 1

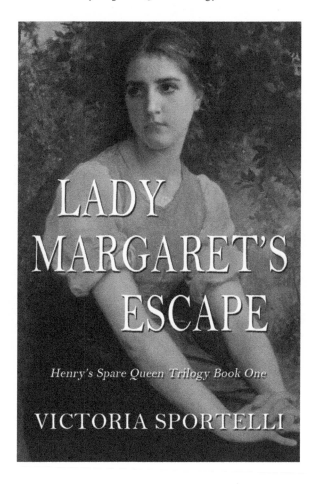

An excerpt

1

Encounters

27 June 1101 A.D.

Morning

"Where is she?" asked Caitlin.

Cook replied, "Left before dawn. With a basket. Wants to be clean for May Day even if she is not allowed to celebrate."

"Too early for the stream to warm much overnight."

"Warm enough. And he's drunk again, so he won't know. Just like last month, she will have to confess getting naked, exposing herself and washing. I hope this time Father Ambroise gives her such a penance as to curtail her. Please stir that pottage for me. I must remove the loaves."

"She will die of ague," worried Caitlin.

"Will not. Too tough. Anyone who wants her dead will have to put a knife into her heart."

"Do not give him ideas! Do not even speak of such things."

"As if I'd speak to that man after what he's done to her!"

Beyond the forest and the estate's eastern border, the sun's tip peeked above the earth. As the church bell rang to announce dawn and Mass, a girl snuck through the gate of the bailey. She crept along the palisade wall toward the kitchen and dashed inside. She breathed a sigh of relief and dropped her basket inside the doorway. She sniffed appreciatively toward the hot loaves of brown bread cooling on the nearby table. She strode to the fireplace mantle to retrieve a jumble of keys and the estate scissors to tie to her girdle. As she picked her apron from a hook and donned it, she heard Cook's warning.

"Best you hurry if you want not to be caught and punished."

The girl ran out the kitchen door, dashed across the bailey down the road, and into the church in time to hear Father Ambroise intone the first words of Mass. She slipped between the two serving girls closest to the entrance. Her first prayer was gratitude to God at not having been caught leaving the compound. After Mass, the priest dismissed parishioners according to each group's standing in the household, the master first, then his family, knights, and finally servants. With the sun now full up in the sky the girl lifted her face to the light to enjoy the coming of a warm day.

Back in the kitchen, the girl asked, "Did he ask for me?"

"No," answered Cook. She turned from ladling the pottage of boiled wheat, oats and leftover bits of squirrel into wooden bowls. "Consider yourself fortunate. Once again." The old woman wagged her finger. "Already seen to your bundle."

"Thank you. The berries already smell good."

"Welcome," came Cook's curt reply.

"Margery!" Sir Charles bellowed from the hall.

124

The girl, called that name by those who commanded her, returned to her role with an effort; she tucked the unruly parts of herself inside. She straightened her clothes before she picked up the tray; her countenance too fell into the lines of blank propriety. As much as she disliked this, there was also a sense of accomplishment at the perfection of her charade. She crossed the space between the kitchen and the hall, reminding herself that she, Margaret, was other than, better than, what this man crudely deemed her. She whisked into the building through the servants' entrance with a platter of steaming bowls and set them on the trestle before she looked toward the head table and curtsied.

I will not react. This is only an act, not the real me. I do this every day.

"Yes, my lord?" Her voice was soft and slow.

"This butter is rancid!" Lord Charles loved to start the day with a complaint. Today it was the chatelaine's turn to suffer his wrath. "When was this muck churned?"

He so enjoys getting worked up, his wrath swelling like a bullfrog's pouch. He doubtless thinks himself very, very important when he is merely petty and cruel. Calm him or he will rampage all morning. "The milk-maid churned it yesterday," came her gentle reply. "I do not consume it, so I did not taste it. Shall I now?"

"No, no. Remove this trash. Bring honey instead."

Margaret curtsied and sweetly replied, "Yes, my lord. Immediately, my lord."

Margaret returned to the kitchen, unlocked the buttery and retrieved the honey pot.

Of course I tasted it after I churned and salted it! Did I not pot, cover and store it as well? Rampaging again, you unwashed blob smelling of stale ale and piss. You are no longer the man Mother once loved.

125

Now each week you slip lower. At the kitchen door Margaret sighed, straightened her back, dipped her littlest finger into the butter and put it into her mouth.

This is fine. I will turn it into a different bowl and serve it with the midday meal; he will know no better.

She returned to the hall, curtsied before the head table and placed the crock and a wooden spoon before her lord. In her mind, she upended it in his lap, though that would be a waste of something more useful than the man. *If only I could give this honey to the little ones or the nursing mothers.*

"Punish the milkmaid. See to it now! And do it my way," Lord Charles ordered. "Leave the honey here; I may want more."

Keeping her eyes down, Margaret nodded and left, contempt simmering around the edges of her thoughts. *Such a strong man you are, able to order a girl hurt!* Margaret stepped carefully across the bailey so as not to kick up dust. *No rain for a fortnight. Our crops need rain now. Please, God, give use the rain we need. Your will, Oh, God, in all things.*

The barn smelled of milk and manure. The maid she sought, a ten-year-old with a round, freckled face and upturned nose, was crooning to her cows, who stared at her with their mild brown eyes.

"He is again on a rampage about butter."

The girl shrunk in horror, her body folding like wheat under a heavy rain. The last time Lord Charles had complained, he had come himself into the stable and had beaten her so badly she could not work for days. Margaret remembered tending to her, her terror that something inside the child had been broken, her hands going again and again to the girl's midsection. Keeping her countenance blank around Lord Charles had been hard.

126

"No, no," Margaret said. "Fear not. He expects me to do it this time. Get ready to howl."

The milkmaid was already whimpering when Sir Charles' head servant walked into the tack area and returned with an old whip handle and a saddle blanket. She looked around and placed the blanket against the outside wall.

"Ready?" Margaret smiled at the girl, silently bidding her be brave. "Come here so we can time my blows and your screams."

"Yes, mistress!" came the girl's eager reply when she saw that the wall and not herself was about to be struck.

A thump against wood.. A whimper.

"Louder," Margaret instructed.

A harder blow. A wail. Another hard blow that echoed in the barn. A howl. A blow heard halfway across the bailey. A scream. The cows moved uneasily in their stalls.

If cows were not so docile, they might attack me for hurting their little mistress.

"Do not overdo it. Now cry."

The girl grinned, "I cannot."

Margaret reached over, grabbed the fleshy part of the girl's forearm, pinched hard and held it. *Does she not know we all must play out this farce? I cannot manage him alone.*

"Ow-u-uch!" Tears welled up in the girl's eyes. She tried to pull away and hurt herself even more. After the milkmaid's tears were flowing, Margaret let go; she felt faintly soiled and at the same time annoyed. *This is not my fault!*

"I am sorry I had to hurt you at all, but you had better show at least one bruise and evidence of having cried. You know what he is like. Now cry all you want. Just remember what you might have gotten."

Margaret returned the blanket and whip handle and walked toward the sobbing child. The girl surprised Margaret with a hug, her thin arms surprisingly strong, her mucky face pressed to the chatelaine's shoulder. She hugged the girl back and kissed her on the forehead, walked through the door and slammed it shut. Margaret yelled inside her head at the lord she served. *I hate you! You horrible, vile man!*

Margaret stopped and stared at what she spotted across the bailey. A knight holding a geldings's reins and a squire with a riding gelding and a pack animal stood before the main door of the hall. The knight was a full head taller than his squire and well muscled. He looked to be in his mid to late twenties, with dark brown hair, cropped for wearing under a helmet. He was clenching a strong jaw; he lifted his chin, and showed a handsome profile. His cloak was serviceable brown, his boots black. Having stopped halfway between barn and kitchen, Margaret admired the man and smiled to see him shifting his feet in annoyance in the ankle-high morning fog.

Norman. Rugged, handsome. Well appointed. Fine horse. Not accustomed to being kept waiting, I wager.

The knight, who felt a twitch in the back of his neck, looked about, and straight into the eyes of a woman wearing the trappings around her waist that informed him of her position. His eyes widened.

Margaret froze. Dark eyes stared back at her. *Why do I feel as if he is undressing me?* Unsettled, the girl ducked her head to break their eye contact and strode quickly toward the kitchen. She missed seeing the knight's smile.

Midnight

Margaret was jolted awake when a dark figure put one hand hard over her mouth and another tightly on the back of her neck. She was pinned face down further with a knee in the small of her back.

A hard-edged whisper demanded, "Woman, what do you know of the king's business?"

She barely managed to shake her head. From the smell of the man, she knew he was not William. The stranger slowly released her mouth.

"Upon my life, I speak to the king--and *only* to him."

The man pulled her to a sitting position and pinned her to the wall with stiff arms. His face was inches from hers.

"Your Royal Highness," Margery whispered in awe as she saw Henry, King of England, in dim firelight.

Through the interior arch that led to the sleeping cubby, he saw two lumps under blankets shift. Margery saw the lumps and a sentinel's back at the kitchen door.

"Back to bed. Cover your heads," Margaret hissed. She waited until Cook and Caitlin obeyed. Speaking barely above a hush, Margaret informed her sovereign lord, "We are now as alone as we can be."

"What do you think you know?" Henry answered in the same hush.

"I know that your queen is again with child. That you seek aid for her."

Suddenly furious, Henry shook the girl's shoulders so hard her head snapped against the wall.

"How?" he demanded.

"In the hall. I heard you. You asked about Sir Charles's Lady Rosamonde, and your eyes changed when you learned she had died.

You lost interest in the rest of the evening. You thought what you had come for was no longer here."

Margaret knew she had only a moment more; she rushed out her words.

"BUT it *is* here. The Lady Rosamonde was known for her power as a healer. Men wanted her because only she stitched up wounds rather than burn them or amputate. You are whole; you need her not for that. Among the Norman ladies she was known for her ability to help women have healthy babes. Babes lived when she delivered them. You have just lost a babe. The queen—you dare not lose this one too."

The king yanked her shoulders forward and then pushed her hard. The girl's head slammed against the wall. Trying to refocus her eyes, Margaret blinked hard several times. The king knocked her head against the wall again; this time not so hard. Chastened, Margaret looked down.

"And…," Henry asked in a hard voice.

"I was...her assistant. I accompanied her many times. I know her ways and her medicines. Since her death, I have delivered the babes on this estate. Except for a shriveled one that had been dead in the womb for weeks, every babe I have delivered since Lady Rosamonde's death is still alive."

"I know nothing of you," King Henry challenged.

"Sir Charles does not allow me to leave his lands," was all she would admit. "Do you want my help with the queen? If you do, I have questions, Your Royal Highness."

Henry slowly released Margaret and shifted so they sat face to face on the sacks. He remained silent for a long moment.

"Please tell me of your babe," Margaret asked politely.

After the Henry answered, she asked him if any had reported the babe's appearance to him. The king was brief; he had seen his dead son himself. The babe was only four months along, almost alive, and perfect except for dark nails. Margaret was moved by the depth of the grief he had stifled in the telling.

"I'm so sorry, My Liege, but I must ask more. When this happened, did Her Royal Highness have a black line under her nails where her skin ends? Did such a line develop before the babe's death?"

Even in the gloom Margaret saw a shock of recognition on her sovereign's face.

"Why, Yes! I saw it when I held her hands. Several of her ladies commented on it as well."

First from Saxon gossip and now from the king's account, Margaret guessed what might have killed his first-born. As she debated whether to speak further, he took the choice from her.

"I command you to tell me what you know."

"Sh-h-h! Your Royal Highness!" Margaret paused. "I am afraid, My King. I am very afraid at what I think."

Henry took up the girl's hands and held them tightly. "I am the King of England. I will protect you. Tell me."

True, *but no one can protect me from you if I am wrong.*

"My King, I fear someone poisoned your queen."

"Poisoned? How?"

Next

Margaret was disgraced and thought her life was over.
After she escapes her father, she bravely endures hard challenges.
Margaret meets a stranger and begins a future she did not expect in

Henry's Spare Queen Trilogy:

Lady Margaret's Escape Book One
Lady Margaret's Challenge Book Two
Lady Margaret's Future Book Three

Lady Margaret's Disgrace: Prequel to
Henry's Spare Queen Trilogy
Release Date: 1 September 2021

Find Victoria online and on social media:
Website: *victoriasportelli.com*
Facebook: facebook.com/victoriasportelli/
Pinterest.com/VictoriaSportelli/
Twitter: @SportelliVic

Dear Reader:

The author will be most grateful
if you leave an honest review online.
Thank you!

Acknowledgements

Without T. M. Evenson's encouragement and support, I would not be an author. This prequel and the trilogy which follows would never have been more than ideas rolling around in my head and stories I would tell her. She is an accomplished writer and computer expert, who introduced me to the program National Novel Writing Month (*NaNoWriMo.org*). She read the first draft of *Lady Margaret Escapes* of the Henry's Spare Queen Trilogy. After she helped me edit it, she taught me about how to be published. Dear Sister, I am forever grateful for all you have taught me and your help all the while you launched *Emergence: The Journey Begins,* the prequel to *The Destiny Saga* and began your first book in the series, *Providence: A New Beginning.*

My beta readers examined an early draft of my writings, and their comments and ideas greatly helped me. Thank you N. Boyt, Ann Burrish, Gail Klein, Christy Lennon, Carol Oakland and Ginger Westberg.

Any "horse sense" in this story comes from my friend Joyce sharing her equine knowledge and my meeting her American saddlebred Gizmo.

Thank you, T. Wiering, for helping me locate Creazzo Publishing.

Glossary

Advent. Period of fasting and reflection, which starts the fourth Sunday before Christmas Day.

Anno Domini. (A.D.): Latin for "in the year of Our Lord." We now use C. E. (Common Era).

anon. Immediately.

bailey. A large area, usually protected by a dry or wet moat, surrounded by a tall wooden or stone wall called a palisade, encircles the hall, keep, kitchen, barrack, chapel, and other buildings where a lord, his family and his retainers reside.

barrack. A building where unmarried knights live.

bedmate. Polite term for any woman a man takes to his bed and uses for his pleasure, whether for a night or longer. Usually a Saxon who had no choice in the matter.

bliaut (a). A Norman-French word. A Norman woman's outer garment to the wrists and ankles, fitted to the elbows for fashion, then flared to the wrist and to hips, then flared below for easy walking, usually wool in winter and linen in summer.

board. The right to be fed and have a table or bench to sleep upon as part of one's service.

boon. A gift or favor granted by one person to another.

C. E. Common Era is the modern term used to describe years. It replaced "A.D." (Anno Domini): Latin for "in the year of Our Lord."

chatelaine. Usually the landholder's wife; she is responsible for everything on the estate except its safety and men's hunting practices.

chemise. A soft undergarment of linen or wool slightly smaller than a bliaut to protect one's skin from chaffing.

Christmastide. The days from Midnight Mass on December 24 through the Epiphany on January 6.

Church. The one, catholic, true religion taught by Jesus the Christ and practiced throughout Western Europe; the pope in Rome was its head; also called the Christian Church.

Confession. A requirement to state one's sins to a priest, receive absolution and to do penance before being permitted to receive Holy Communion.

courses. The monthly cycle of a woman losing blood because she is not with child.. While a girl may be contracted to a marriage, the wedding may not be blessed and she may not be bedded until her courses come.

dais. In a hall, a platform two to four steps high upon which sits a table and benches, stools or chairs and from which the lord of the estate and his family dine and rule.

ditch woman. A girl/woman whose father/husband has thrown her out of her family for unacceptable behavior, such as disobedience, having sexual relations outside marriage, running away, etc. She lives in fear of her life because anyone can do anything to her; she is a pariah.

Epiphany (January 6). The twelfth day after Christmas, believed to be the day the Magi visited the Christ child and gave him gifts; a time of gift giving and feasting.

excommunicate. A severe penalty for a gross offense to the Church which results in a person's inability to receive the sacraments or be buried in holy ground. One must still attend Mass. The penalty is reversible if one repents, goes to Confession, completes a penance and changes one's ways. One is then readmitted to the Body of Christ's followers and to His Church.

feudalism. All of England was owned by the king. He portioned out some of it to be held by those beneath him, who worked and protected it on his behalf. A barren held vast tracts of land and answered directly to the king. With royal permission, a baron could separate his lands into earldoms and raise a lord or knight to that station. In turn, either the earl or baron could then assign land within an earldom to a knight who could then marry because he was a landholder. Each rank owed military service and taxes to the station directly above his.

fostered, fostering. An exchange of children so they may be trained to specific skills and become aware of other families on other estates. Sometimes used as a prelude to marriage.

girl. Any unmarried female, no matter her age.

Grand Crusade. In 1095 Pope Urban II called all of Christendom to a crusade to free Eastern Christians from Turkish rule and to take possession of the Holy City of Jerusalem. When Jerusalem fell to the Turks in 1147, a second Crusade was called and the custom of numbering the Crusades began; this one was then renamed the First Crusade.

gunna. A Saxon word for a long-sleeved woolen dress worn to the ankles and fastened to the body with a belt. Most Saxon women owned only one, which they wore until they were annually given cloth by their lord to make another one in preparation for Easter. Similar to a bliaut, but straight from shoulder to hem.

hall. The building where the Norman members of an estate dine and conduct business.

Holy Communion. A piece of bread and a sip of wine transformed into the body and blood of Jesus the Christ by a priest during Mass. The ceremony unites all of Christendom, and only those in good standing with the Church may partake in it.

keep. A square building usually of stone, sometimes of wood, where the Norman lord and his family may flee for safety if his estate is attacked and his bailey is breached; generally they live there.

knight errant. Designates a fighter in arms who serves or is hired by one of rank without his being given land, called "Sir" out of politeness but bears no rank.

knight landed or just **knight.** A knight errant who has been given land and who may now marry; he serves a man of a noble rank above his; his is the lowest noble title during these times (See "titles").

Lent. Forty days of fasting and prayer from Monday through Saturday, begun on Ash Wednesday and culminating on Easter Sunday.

litter. A curtained and canopied conveyance for a lady of rank. She sits or lies among cushions, blankets and furs on a wooden plank while the device is attached to a horse front and back. No real lady rides unless she must.

mantle. A hoodless, sleeveless warm outer covering worn by men and women (what we call a cape).

mark. A measure of money equivalent to 160 pennies. In 1096, 10,000 Marks was 1.6 million pennies when two pennies bought a boar pig, one penny bought a sow, and piglets were two for a penny.

marriage chest. A wooden chest, carved or plain, into which a girl places the linens she has hemmed and all manner of clothing, fabrics, household goods and items she has made or acquired and will take with her to her new home. During the 20th century, it was called a "hope chest."

Mass. A religious service lead by a priest or higher member of the Church in which all Christians attend and those in good standing with the Church receive Holy Communion as a way of uniting all Christendom and keeping its members faithful.

May Day. May 1.

Michaelmas. September 29.

Midsummer. The summer solstice, usually June 21 or 22, depending on the moon cycles that year.

Millennium (The). Believed to be 1000 AD, though some argued it was actually 1001AD; the time the Church believed Jesus the Christ would return.

mortal sin. A misdeed that will cause your soul be sent to Hell if it is not forgiven and more serious than a venial sin, which is a misdeed and a minor offense against God and/or the Church.

New Forest. An area southwest of Winchester, England, formed by King William II because he wanted easy access to a forest to hunt deer and boar. He displaced several prominent lords from prime property and gave them lands elsewhere, destroyed their buildings and had trees planted.

Norman. Both the name of the group and the language the Normans of England and Normandy spoke during the twelfth century. We now call the language Old Norman-French.

palisade. The wall of wooden timbers or of stone, which surrounds the bailey and all within; usually has either a d dry or wet moat around it for further protection and only one gate for entrance.

parchment. Sheep skin that has been pounded thin and stretched and upon which records are written.

pariah. A person who has done something so awful that all of society shuns her/him; an individual who has no social protections.

penance. Prayers and good deeds that must be completed before one's sins are expunged and before one can receive Holy Communion during Mass.

Percheron. A horse, usually black but sometimes gray, from Perche, a region which is now in northwest France.

pottage. Soaked grains, into which can be thrown leftover vegetables and meats, that is cooked and turned into a soup/stew served in the morning. This word was later changed to porridge.

pulses. Most commonly peas or other pod vegetables that grow quickly and can be eaten fresh or dried. Remember the song/verse: "Peas porridge hot. Peas porridge cold. Peas porridge in the pot nine days old."

rank. See titles. Within each title, men are ranked according to how much land they hold, their level of wealth, and how the royals favor them. Wives, sons, and daughters hold the same rank as the head of their household.

reeve. On an estate, a man who has been elected each January by his fellow Saxons to oversee all the assigning of land, planting, growing, and harvesting of crops. Traditionally, he may elected only three times before another man must be chosen.

rib. See wedding rib.

Saxon. Both the people of England who were invaded in 1066 by King William I (the Conqueror) and the language they spoke. We now call their language Old Saxon.

seneschal. The man in charge of the estate who follows his lord's orders and the chatelaine's instructions; like the foreman of a ranch.

serfs (see villeins). Term for the persons tied to the land owned by the king, barons, earls, and lords, as part of the feudalism system common on the European continent. Usually they are not free, but they are not bought or sold as if they were slaves.

shift (a). A soft undergarment of linen or wool slightly smaller than a bliaut to protect one's skin from chaffing.

simples. Ointments, creams, powders, and other simple remedies for a variety of illnesses and ailments; most use pig fat as a base.

sodomite. A man who loves/has sexual relations with another man.

stone (a). A unit of weight equal to 14 pounds.

titles. Royal: King/Queen

Prince/Princess

Noble* — Baron/Baroness (called Lady)

Earl/Countess (called Lady)

Lord (sometimes addressed as Sir/Sirrah)/Lady

Sir(Sirrah)/Lady (a knight who owns land)

*During these years titles of address were fluid. All the nobles except for knights landed could be—and often were—addressed as "Lord"—even the earls, and many times the barons/earls and lords were informally addressed as "Sir."

three days' time. The time between judgement and execution; required by the Church so clergy had time to save the person's soul and to prepare her/him for death.

trial by combat. Under Norman law, only an accused Norman could fight to prove his innocence. He chose the weapons and rules. If the accused won the contest, a formal trial was never held because God had protected the righteous one and made him victorious.The Lord God has proven the accuser wrong.

vassal. Under the feudal system, any person who holds land and owes taxes, homage, fealty and/or military service to an individual of higher rank; in England all are vassals except the king.

villeins (see serfs). Term used in England for those tied to the land, who are not free.

walkway. Structure attached behind the palisade upon which guards may stand and defend the bailey.

wedding rib. A strip of woven, lightweight cloth 3-6 inches wide used as decorative trim on clothing or is wrapped around a woman's long hair when she wears it in two braids. Thin ribs are often woven into braids for decoration. We now call them ribbons.

warrior priest. A priest who has been trained as a swordsman and fighter and who guards the Church's property. After King William II prevented Archbishop Anselm from appointing bishops and took their lands for the income, several bishops created these men to protect themselves and their bishoprics.

wattle and daub. A form of construction using softened sticks woven tougher (wattle) and a mud of dirt, straw and other debris (daub) to form walls of a hut that is then roofed with thatch. A common home for Saxons during this era.

wench. A female servant, whether girl or woman.

About the Author

V. C. Sportelli's passion is 11th and early 12th century English history, folklore, and writings. Her stories of Lady Margaret, King Henry and Queen Matilda reflect their times and struggles. Lady Margaret fights against her era's restrictions of women as she is determined to find her own way in the world. The king and queen face fierce opposition to their rule. As Ms. Sportelli researched King Henry's early years, she found compelling his conflicts with the Normans and the Saxons. She has concluded that Henry I of England was an under-rated king who did much to turn the Norman army of invasion into citizens of law.

A life-long anglophile, Ms. Sportelli is fascinated by England and its people. In addition to traveling throughout England, she has been to the places she writes about. One of her most exciting finds is in the hall to the Queen's Wing of the Great Hall, which is all that remains of a castle in Winchester. Hanging there is a photograph of a medieval royal treasury chest historians believe King William II and King Henry I might have used. The chest is now stored in London.

Thank you for reading *Lady Margaret's Disgrace*.
I hope you enjoyed it. If you did...

1   Help other people find this book by writing an honest review online.

2   Come like my facebook page at *www.facebook.com/victoria*sportelli/

3   Keep reading about Margaret's adventures in *Lady Margaret's Escape* where she meets King Henry and helps Queen Matilda.

Made in the USA
Las Vegas, NV
27 November 2022

60470613R00094